# THROUGH THE CLOCK'S WORKINGS

Edited by Amy Barker

SYDNEY UNIVERSITY PRESS

Published 2009 by Sydney University Press
SYDNEY UNIVERSITY PRESS
University of Sydney Library
www.sydney.edu.au/sup

National Library of Australia Cataloguing-in-Publication entry
Title:           Through the clock's workings / editor Amy Barker.
ISBN:            9781920899325 (pbk.)
Subjects:        Short stories.
Other Authors/Contributors:
                 Barker, Amy 1978-
Dewey Number:    808.831

Printed in Australia

# Contents

# Foreword

Most creative disciplines have grappled with the concept of remix. For mediums such as film and music entire communities of appropriation (legal or otherwise) have emerged. Artists whose creative practice is contingent to the adaptation of, and addition to, existing creative products populate this space. But other creative disciplines are practically devoid of this creative technique.

Read/Write has traditionally been a dichotomy in literature. The author is on one side of the production process, toiling away in solitude to produce the manuscript which is read by many, in solitude. But is there a more collaborative space for literature? Can your pages be Read&Write? Remix My Lit, a Brisbane-based, international remixable literature project thought so.

A joint venture of the ARC Centre for Excellence in Creative Industries and Innovation and Story of the Future at the Australia Council for the Arts, the project applied the lessons learned from music and film remixing to literature. It has explored where remix fits into literature by providing a space within the discipline to encourage and foster a community and culture of remix at: www.remixmylit.com. The project would like to acknowledge and thank Professor Stuart Cunningham, Professor Brian Fitzgerald and Therese Fingleton for their support in this endeavour.

Established Australian authors contributed short stories, which were released under a Creative Commons Attribution-NonCommercial-Share Alike licence. Young and emerging writers were then invited to remix the stories, while acknowledging the original author, ensuring the remix was not for commercial use, and making their new work available for others to remix. This anthology has brought together the original stories with the best of the remixes by young and emerging writers to create a world first: a remixed and remixable short fiction anthology. With these imaginative remixes full of wordplay, wit and wonder, *Through the Clock's Workings* brings contemporary Australian short fiction thoroughly up to date.

Amy Barker, Remix My Lit Project Leader
& Elliott Bledsoe, Creative Commons Project Officer
Brisbane, February 2009.

# Alchymical Romance
## Lee Battersby

*Nigredo*

The problem was, he had never loved her. They both knew it, even in those moments after orgasm, when they leaned into each other and persuaded themselves that it meant more than shared sweat and another notch on a mental bedpost. Another boast for his mates, if only he had any.

Now she was gone, and it wasn't her absence that kept him from re-entering the world. The thought of it wearied him before he started. The long, dreary process of nightclubs, and blind dates, and turning up for dinners with colleagues to find an extra female present and the only empty chair directly opposite. The whole thing was such a drudge, and she'd have to be a sexual athlete of Olympic proportions to make up for the love he wouldn't feel for her. Too much trouble for the few weeks before her presence began to drain him of everything he held dear. Then she'd be gone, and the bar would be raised another notch for whomever came next, and where would it all lead him? A woman with superhuman flexibility and the perverse nature of an Indian God, perhaps. A woman made of fingertips and tongues, with no sense of shame.

And he still wouldn't love her.

He sat at his kitchen table, sipped coffee, and stared over his newspaper at the busy street beyond his window. There was no way around it. He couldn't face the real world. He had lived too long with reality. He raised a hand to his neck and ran fingertips along the network of tiny puncture marks criss-crossing the skin at the base of his jaw. He would have to visit Sir Million.

He plucked a set of keys from the hook by the phone and rubbed his thumb across the silver dog tag. There was a time when he could rejoice in the sensation the stamped letters made under his thumb, delight in the ripple of cold, rolled edges against his skin. Now: nothing. He felt nothing. He sighed, and pocketed the keys.

The streets north of Perth wither and die in the winter rain, leaving behind slick tarmac and an occasional oasis of sodium light. Residents close their curtains and hide before televisions, ignoring the rolls of thunder as best they can. Markus' black Audi slid along unnoticed, undisturbed, a metal shark cruising an empty ocean. Markus barely noticed the lack of humanity. Their absence meant only a lessening of white noise, a drop in the background level of static, a slight reinforcement of the link between his subconscious and the muted hum of the city. He glided along black tracks: a tiny spark within a vast, dormant machine; a single atom within a city-wide accelerator.

He hit the end of the freeway without seeing another car, turned away from the bridge, past late night construction works, and away from the centre of Joondalup, devoid of personality without its semi-permanent cast of shoppers; just an empty façade of shop fronts and parking lots, glistening clean in the aftermath of the evening's downpour. A right at the lights, and he pushed past the suburban sprawl, attention fixed upon the promise of overgrown country roads to come, and the moment of pure solitude before Sir Million's driveway.

After half an hour he left the coast, and soon found himself on the lonely road leading northwards from Wanneroo into the countryside. Trees formed a tunnel of outstretched fingers at the periphery of his headlights. Before he could get used to the ghostly burrow and decide to follow it into forever, Markus spied the entrance to Sir Million's driveway. He slid into the oncoming lane, took the turn without slowing, and jounced up the dirt lane as fast as the Audi's suspension would allow. He pulled up before the house with a squeal of brakes, a ghost of dust settling in his wake. Markus sat with the lights out and listened to the ticking of the car's cooling engine. There should have been *some* movement from outside, some noise in response to his arrival. An explosion of birds from the surrounding trees, a barking dog, even a light inside a window. Instead, nothing. Animals knew better than to come near the residence, Markus thought without amusement. With no better alternative, he opened the car door and stepped out.

The slamming door sounded supernaturally loud in the dead air. Markus surveyed the house. It had shrunk since his last visit. He'd expected that. Sir Million had stumbled across the ruins of the homestead some ninety years ago, if you believed the man- a gutted shell of broken masonry with only ghosts for occupants. Bit by bit, using whatever flotsam the universe deposited before him, he had rebuilt it to his own design, obsessively refining and shaping until every room, every angle, had reflected his own arcane needs. The man had shrunk as he'd aged, and the house had followed him. Now it was little more than a shanty. Bare wood boards patched together bricks of countless shades; glassless windows peered out at whatever angle they had been forced into the gaps; animal bones, wire, feathers, a rainbow assortment of bottles. Nothing had been spared. The house crouched upon bare soil like an abandoned engine. *No wonder nature avoids this place*, Markus thought for the hundredth time. *It's like a lunatic's dream catcher. Which*, he reflected as he tested his weight on an unfamiliar porch step, *it is.*

The front door swung open as he raised his fist to knock. Markus stepped into the darkened hallway.

'Hello?'

No answer. Light framed a door at the far end of the hall. He was almost upon it when it, too, swung open. A lumpen silhouette stood in the light.

'Markus de Brant! I knew it would be you!'

The silhouette reached out misshapen arms, grabbed Markus by the wrists and dragged him into the light.


*Albedo*

Idly, Markus noted the whirr and click of clockwork.

Sir Million turned from him, making his way across a room overgrown with a profusion of esoteric constructions: pipes that began in one box and ended in another, if at all; dials that spun and whirred; cabinets in a myriad of shapes, covered with inscriptions, crackling with sparks at odd moments; cups; plates; cutlery, bent and deformed; statuettes; mummies both human and otherwise; painting, plans, and blueprints; and over everything a flow of detritus and flotsam the nature of which Markus could not begin to guess. The whole effect was one of arcane disorder, as if some key to understanding lurked just out of Markus' grasp, and only with it could he begin to divine a purpose from his surroundings.

Sir Million stopped by an overstuffed sofa, crammed between a dozen empty canvasses and something that could have been either an iron maiden or cappuccino machine, depending on the angle from which it was viewed. He cleared a space by the simple expedient of dumping everything on the floor, and patted a cushion, arm jerking spasmodically.

'Come. Sit.'

Markus studied the old man. He had grown younger since their last meeting. Metal plates covered large areas of his body, his skin smoothed out and neatly tucked behind them. Assemblages of rods and pistons surrounded his knee and hip joints, and everything was connected to a small engine that crouched on his back and contributed to his lumpy, toad-like shape. Steam hissed whenever he moved. He stared at Markus expectantly. Markus coughed.

'You've changed.'

'Necessary. Big explosion. Lost bits. You'd have known if you visited.' His head twitched to the side. 'Still, worth it. Look.'

A window ran the length of the far wall, opening out onto a back yard more bedlam than garden. A bench table crouched underneath, back almost broken by the weight of tubing that covered it. At regular intervals, liquid dripped from openings into petri dishes filled with piles of coloured powder.

'Uranium,' Sir Million said. 'Strontium, mescaline, heroin, saffron.' He laughed, a sound like the clearing of pipes. 'The Alchymical wedding, in all its most lovely forms. Gold is for amateurs.' He turned his mechanical gaze upon Markus. 'Now. You.'

Markus shrugged. 'It's not –'

'Not working?'

'No.'

Sir Million raised himself from the seat, stalked over to Markus, began to prod him here and there about the torso.

'You don't feel? Not a thing? Nothing penetrates?'

'Physical things.' Markus shrugged again. 'Pain, cold, you know. Nothing emotional.'

'No laughter? Fear?' He snapped his fingers before Markus' eyes, peered into his ear, up his nose. 'Love?'

'No.' Markus gazed steadily out the window, at the bombsite of weeds and rubble beyond. 'No love.'

'And this is important?'

A rat peered at Markus from the window of a rusted car, then withdrew into the dark. 'I don't know.'

'But you want to.'

'Still.'

Sir Million turned away, walked to the window, and stared at the sky.

'One hundred and sixty five years, seven months, three days, twenty one hours, several minutes, assorted seconds. A long time. Still you all come. Problems, problems, problems. No matter the country, or the time. You all come.'

'I'm sorry.'

'No.'

Markus bit his lip. 'No. I guess not.'

'If you were, the problem would not exist.'

'No.'

Sir Million returned his gaze to the room. He clapped his hands, a sound like cymbals. 'Still. If you did not come, the solution would not be found. I have never failed. Never. Not with Queens, nor Fuehrers, nor Godmakers. In what do you work now?'

'Work? Um. I was in advertising, last time. I'm in web design now. Contract work.'

'A web designer. Not worth becoming my first failure. Not after Queens and ...' Sir Million waved his hand. 'And so on and so on. This time, this time, I will find what you need.'

'I don't even know *what* I want any more.'

'I don't care about want. Now sit.'

He indicated a chair in the darkest recess of the room, a complicated web of wires perched upon it like a crown. Markus sat, wiggled his backside around until he was comfortable.

Sir Million threaded a long tube onto a hypodermic, swabbed a spot on Markus' temple, and carefully inserted the needle into the skin. Markus sucked air between his teeth. Previous experience kept him from flinching. Sir Million drew off several millilitres of milky fluid, and frowned.

'So little left. This will be the last time, old fellow. The last time for us both. You are bereft of essence.'

'So soon?'

'So soon? Pish. Nobody bothers me as you do. You are quite drained, my boy. Drawn dry. This *is* the last time.'

He withdrew the needle and placed it to one side. Moving about the machine, he encased Markus in the cage of wire. Countless tiny spikes pressed against his skin at head, face, throat and wrist, points nestling inside the healed over puncture wounds that littered his body.

'One more time to capture your dreams,' Sir Million said. 'One more time to bring them to life. Don't blink.' He clanked across the room to rest his hand atop a large, tape-wrapped lever set into the wall. 'This is going to hurt.'

Markus stared at the world outside the window. With a sigh of expelled steam, Sir Million lowered the lever, and the world turned black.


*Rubedo*

The problem was, he could never have loved her, no matter how much he needed it. No matter how many bodies filled his bed, or whatever drugs, blades or fluids he used to batter his nerve endings, the core of him remained indifferent. Nothing reached inside. The void remained empty, pressing against his organs, deadening everything it touched. Nothing had changed, not in all the months since his visit to Sir Million. Not since then, and not in all the years before. It was not that the failures proved so disastrous. It was knowing the inevitability of failure, and still being compelled to try.

The taxi arrived, the lover departed, and a small interval of peace descended. Again, and again, and again.

Today, however, a change: the taxi was gone, and a courier van filled the driveway. A uniformed figure approached, knocked on the front door. Markus signed the proffered form, received the brown-wrapped package. A flat box, perhaps four inches thick, long and wide enough that he chose to lean it against the arm of his sofa rather than attempt to lift it onto the coffee table. He curled his fingers over the top flap and pulled, revealing the contents in one long tear of cardboard.

A mirror, simply framed, reflective surface gleaming a dull brass in the light from the single lamp. A small sheet of something like thick paper was taped to its surface. Markus fingered it. A spark of something tickled him inside. The sheet was not paper, but vellum– smooth and supple beneath his fingers, slick as he pulled it from its mooring. He recognised Sir Million's rounded, feminine hand in the letters stained into its surface. He read.

> *Dear Fellow,*
> *A surprise. Not what you expected. There was so little of you left. So few drops of essence. Not enough to transmute blood or dreams. Enough to spread over a surface. Enough, I hope, to show you. What? Who knows? A mirror made of you, dear Markus. Let it not fail.*
> *M o'C*

Markus ran a finger over the mirror's surface, frowning. It was soft and warm, sticky, not at all the cold, smooth metal he had expected. In the mirror, his doppelganger frowned and removed its finger from the glass. Markus bent, and peered closely. The image was dark, its outline vague and wavering. He stood and recovered the lamp from the far corner of the room, set it upon the coffee table, and knelt before the mirror again. The light worked- he saw himself, the details of the room stark behind him. Still, the image bore soft edges, almost out of focus, as if a million tiny imperfections caught the light and diffused it. A fault of the odd surface, Markus decided. A flaw in his essence.

There was something else wrong with the image, something he could not quite put his finger on. Markus traced his outline. There he was, in the centre of the glass, in his shirt and trousers, and with a look on his face that countless women had referred to as the final straw. The lamp was there, casting its light. The coffee table, the curtains ... there. Behind him, to the right. A figure. A dim smudge where he should be able to see to the wall. As Markus watched it came closer, became clearer. A woman. There was a woman. Markus spun away from the mirror with a gasp, then stopped short. The room was empty. The coffee table, the lamp, the curtains. Nothing else. He turned again to the glass. She was there, almost touching his shoulder. Markus reached out behind him, felt nothing.

'What the hell?'

There was more, now, Markus saw. A fault with the woman, something wrong, or missing. She was beautiful, breathtakingly so: short without appearing small; curvaceous; her breasts the perfect size to balance the swell of her hips; elfin features atop a long neck; suntanned skin the colour of lightly burnished bronze; short bobbed hair curled around delicate ears. Her almond eyes met his. She smiled, and in that smile lay all the joys that had avoided him for as long as he could remember. Markus gasped. A bolt of heat struck the centre of his chest, tearing his breath away. The woman stepped in front of the mirror-Markus and raised her hand. She was perfect, as perfect as any desire he could ever have. And exposed to his gaze as she was, with nothing between them but the surface of the mirror, the light from two lamps playing across her, front and back, Markus saw the wrongness he had been unable to place. Her skin was not just the colour of bronze. It *was* bronze.

The woman in the mirror was made of bronze.

They stayed that way for several minutes, staring at each other across a gulf of space and understanding. Then, with a smile so sweet it made the void inside Markus ache, she raised one perfectly forged hand, and beckoned him: closer, closer. Markus fell to both knees, inches from the mirror. Without knowing why, he raised his hand and pressed it against the sticky surface, like a prison inmate in an interview booth, desperate for the touch of a visiting lover. The surface resisted him briefly, then his hand sank into it, deeper than the millimetres-thick plane. He let go a shout of surprise. On the other side of the image, his hand appeared. Only it was not his hand but a simulacrum, in every detail a perfect imitation of his own, forged from glinting bronze.

Markus wiggled his fingers, and the bronze hand in the mirror did the same. He clenched his fist, and watched the metal fingers curl over until they pressed against their palm. He pulled back, and his arm came out of the glass. The hand slid backwards until the heel was on one side and the fingers were on the other. Markus stared at it, then leaned forward again.

'How? I don't ...' But of course, he *did* know. It was Sir Million, and his essence, and the need that had been drawn out of him – transformed, transfigured, given shape. He looked into the perfect eyes of the bronze woman. She reached out, and her hand nestled inside his.

And suddenly, just like that, the barrier that surrounded his void was ruptured, and into the breach poured ... he didn't know, didn't have the words, but it was hot as blood, and it stung, and the emptiness inside him drank and drank and he was crying and laughing and so ... so ...

'Oh, oh, God. Oh, God.' He brought his free hand to his face, and wept into it. 'Oh, God.'

And slowly, slowly, the first, boiling rush of emotion thickened, settled, until the void was full and only gentle waves lapped at the edges. Markus raised his head, drew the back of his hand across his face, tears and snot mingling in a long streak. He sniffed, brought his breathing under control.

'Oh, God,' he said to the woman behind the mirror. 'Is this what it feels like? Oh, God. Do I love you?'

She smiled, and pulled on his hand, drawing him closer to the surface of the glass. Markus resisted, looked around – at the room, the furnishings, the fixtures. Nothing here, he realised, nothing that isn't beyond the mirror. Nothing that isn't replicated. He turned his gaze back to the glass, and the one thing he could not find anywhere else.

'But what if ...?'

He paused. What if what? He looked at himself in the mirror. What happens to him, he thought, if I'm there too? Does he disappear? Do I? And if I disappear, will anyone notice? Will they care?

And he realised: it doesn't matter. None of it does. Whatever happened, he would not be alone. Whatever happened, she would be beside him, and if not her, then someone, and he would love her.

He would love her. And for that small fact, that one small fact, he would risk the answer to any question.

Smiling, crying, happy, Markus bent forward and leaned beyond the mirror.

# Alchymical Romance [Baum-bastic Mix]
## Matthew Lowe

The metal man raised his fist to knock, but the front door swung on its own.

'Hello?'

The room was empty. The four travellers stepped into the darkened hallway and the door slammed behind them, sounding supernaturally loud in the dead air.

'Back so soon?' said a Voice. It seemed to come from everywhere and nowhere. 'I knew it would be you!'

He laughed, a sound like the clearing of pipes.

'Please, Sir,' said the girl. 'We have come for our reward.'

'What of the woman with skin the colour of bronze?' he said, with a sigh of expelled steam.

'Transformed to liquid.'

'How? I don't ... Why do you seek me?' he said, after a small interval.

The Animal raised his head, brought his breathing under control. Although he was scared, he realised it didn't matter. None of it did. Whatever happened, he would not be alone. Whatever happened, she would be beside him, and if not her, then someone else. And for that small fact, that one small fact, he would risk the answer to any question.

'Please, Sir,' he said. 'What about your promise?'

'Yes,' said the man of straw. 'I want –'

'I don't care about want,' shouted the Voice. 'Nobody bothers me as you do! I am Oz, the Great and Terrible! Not some lunatic's dream catcher.'


The travellers leaned into each other as an explosion of steam ran past them. The metal man fell to his knees.

'What now?' he cried.

Nothing had changed. The void remained empty. Still he would not love.

There was something wrong, something the travellers could not quite put a finger on. They stayed that way for several minutes, staring at each other across a gulf of space and understanding. From the far corner of the room there was the sudden sound of a barking dog. At the far end of the hall light framed a door. A lumpen figure stood in the light. A dim smudge fighting the curtains. He let go a shout of surprise.

'No,' he said. 'It's not ...'

With no better alternative, the man opened the curtains and stepped out. The Animal grabbed him by the wrists and dragged him into the light. There he was, in his shirt and trousers, a look of shame taped to his face.


'Problems, problems, problems. You all come. I don't know.' Oz walked to the window, and stared at the sky. 'No matter. I will find what you need. One more time to capture your dreams,' said the Wizard. 'One more time to bring them to life.'

The Wizard stalked over to the metal man, began to prod him about the torso. He raised a hand to his neck and ran fingertips along the network of tiny puncture marks criss-crossing the skin at the base of his jaw.

'You don't feel? Not a thing?' He peered into his ear, up his nose. 'No love? Nothing penetrates?'

'No,' the metal man said. 'I'm bereft of essence. There are ... lost bits.'

'Pish,' said the old man, 'Too much trouble. Love is for amateurs.'

The metal man gazed steadily ahead.

'But you want to try?' the Wizard sighed. 'This is still going to hurt you.'

He indicated a chair in the darkest recess of the room. The metal man sat. Metal plates covered his body, his skin smoothed out and neatly tucked behind them. Assemblages of rods and pistons surrounded his knee and hip joints, and everything was connected to a small engine that hissed whenever he moved. He stared at Oz expectantly.

Oz bent and peered closely. He curled his fingers over the top flap and pulled. It was soft and warm, sticky, not at all the cold, smooth metal he had expected. He reached inside, cleared a space, carefully inserted a flat box, perhaps four inches thick. Then carefully, without a word, he withdrew his arm.

There was the whirr and click of clockwork. The metal man stood gently.

A spark of something tickled him inside. Slowly, slowly, the first boiling rush of emotion thickened, settled. Suddenly, just like that, a bolt of heat struck the centre of his chest, tearing the steam from his pistons. It was hot as blood, and it stung, and the emptiness inside drank and drank until the void was full and alchymical waves lapped at the core of him.

'Oh, God,' he said to the girl. 'Is this what it feels like? Oh, God. Do I love you?'

# Alchymical Romance [Gender Exchange Remix]
## Sarah Xu

*Nigredo*

The problem was, she had never loved him. They both knew it, even in those moments after orgasm, when they leaned into each other and persuaded themselves that it meant more than shared sweat and another notch on a mental bedpost. Another boast for her mates, if only she had any.

Now he was gone, and it wasn't his absence that kept her from re-entering the world. The thought of it wearied her before she started. The long, dreary process of nightclubs, and blind dates, and turning up for dinners with colleagues to find an extra male present and the only empty chair directly opposite. The whole thing was such a drudge, and he'd have to be a sexual athlete of Olympic proportions to make up for the love she wouldn't feel for him. Too much trouble for the few weeks before his presence began to drain her of everything she held dear. Then he'd be gone, and the bar would be raised another notch for whomever came next, and where would it all lead her? A man with superhuman flexibility and the perverse nature of an Indian God, perhaps. A man made of fingertips and tongues, with no sense of shame.

And she still wouldn't love him.

She sat at her kitchen table, sipped coffee, and stared over her newspaper at the busy street beyond her window. There was no way around it. She couldn't face the real world. She had lived too long with reality. She raised a hand to her neck and ran fingertips along the network of tiny puncture marks criss-crossing the skin at the base of her jaw. She would have to visit Lady Million.

She plucked a set of keys from the hook by the phone and rubbed her thumb across the silver dog tag. There was a time when she could rejoice in the sensation the stamped letters made under her thumb, delight in the ripple of cold, rolled edges against her skin. Now: nothing. She felt nothing. She sighed, and pocketed the keys.

The streets north of Perth wither and die in the winter rain, leaving behind slick tarmac and an occasional oasis of sodium light. Residents close their curtains and hide before televisions, ignoring the rolls of thunder as best they can. Margaret's black Audi slid along unnoticed, undisturbed, a metal shark cruising an empty ocean. Margaret barely noticed the lack of humanity. Their absence meant only a lessening of white noise, a drop in the background level of static, a slight reinforcement of the link between her subconscious and the muted hum of the city. She glided along black tracks: a tiny spark within a vast, dormant machine; a single atom within a city-wide accelerator.

She hit the end of the freeway without seeing another car, turned away from the bridge, past late night construction works, and away from the centre of Joondalup, devoid of personality without its semi-permanent cast of shoppers; just an empty façade of shop fronts and parking lots, glistening clean in the aftermath of the evening's downpour. A right at the lights, and she pushed past the suburban sprawl, attention fixed upon the promise of overgrown country roads to come, and the moment of pure solitude before Lady Million's driveway.

After half an hour she left the coast, and soon found herself on the lonely road leading northwards from Wanneroo into the countryside. Trees formed a tunnel of outstretched fingers at the periphery of her headlights. Before she could get used to the ghostly burrow and decide to follow it into forever, Margaret spied the entrance to Lady Million's driveway. She slid into the oncoming lane, took the turn without slowing, and jounced up the dirt lane as fast as the Audi's suspension would allow. She pulled up before the house with a squeal of brakes, a ghost of dust settling in her wake. Margaret sat with the lights out and listened to the ticking of the car's cooling engine. There should have been some movement from outside, some noise in response to her arrival. An explosion of birds from the surrounding trees, a barking dog, even a light inside a window. Instead, nothing. Animals knew better than to come near the residence, Margaret thought without amusement. With no better alternative, she opened the car door and stepped out.

The slamming door sounded supernaturally loud in the dead air. Margaret surveyed the house. It had shrunk since her last visit. She'd expected that. Lady Million had stumbled across the ruins of the homestead some ninety years ago, if you believed the woman – a gutted shell of broken masonry with only ghosts for occupants. Bit by bit, using whatever flotsam the universe deposited before her, she had rebuilt it to her own design, obsessively refining and shaping until every room, every angle, had reflected her own arcane needs. The woman had shrunk as she'd aged, and the house had followed her. Now it was little more than a shanty. Bare wood boards patched together bricks of countless shades; glassless windows peered out at whatever angle they had been forced into the gaps; animal bones, wire, feathers, a rainbow assortment of bottles. Nothing had been spared. The house crouched upon bare soil like an abandoned engine. No wonder nature avoids this place, Margaret thought for the hundredth time. It's like a lunatic's dream catcher. Which, she reflected as she tested her weight on an unfamiliar porch step, it is.

The front door swung open as she raised her fist to knock. Margaret stepped into the darkened hallway.

'Hello?'

No answer. Light framed a door at the far end of the hall. She was almost upon it when it, too, swung open. A lumpen silhouette stood in the light.

'Margaret de Brant! I knew it would be you!'

The silhouette reached out misshapen arms, grabbed Margaret by the wrists and dragged her into the light.

*Albedo*

Idly, Margaret noted the whirr and click of clockwork.

Lady Million turned from her, making her way across a room overgrown with a profusion of esoteric constructions: pipes that began in one box and ended in another, if at all; dials that spun and whirred; cabinets in a myriad of shapes, covered with inscriptions, crackling with sparks at odd moments; cups; plates; cutlery, bent and deformed; statuettes; mummies both human and otherwise; painting, plans, and blueprints; and over everything a flow of detritus and flotsam the nature of which Margaret could not begin to guess. The whole effect was one of arcane disorder, as if some key to understanding lurked just out of Margaret's grasp, and only with it could she begin to divine a purpose from her surroundings.

Lady Million stopped by an overstuffed sofa, crammed between a dozen empty canvasses and something that could have been either an iron maiden or cappuccino machine, depending on the angle from which it was viewed. She cleared a space by the simple expedient of dumping everything on the floor, and patted a cushion, arm jerking spasmodically.

'Come. Sit.'

Margaret studied the old woman. She had grown younger since their last meeting. Metal plates covered large areas of her body, her skin smoothed out and neatly tucked behind them. Assemblages of rods and pistons surrounded her knee and hip joints, and everything was connected to a small engine that crouched on her back and contributed to her lumpy, toad-like shape. Steam hissed whenever she moved. She stared at Margaret expectantly. Margaret coughed.

'You've changed.'

'Necessary. Big explosion. Lost bits. You'd have known if you visited.' Her head twitched to the side. 'Still, worth it. Look.'

A window ran the length of the far wall, opening out onto a back yard more bedlam than garden. A bench table crouched underneath, back almost broken by the weight of tubing that covered it. At regular intervals, liquid dripped from openings into petri dishes filled with piles of coloured powder.

'Uranium,' Lady Million said. 'Strontium, mescaline, heroin, saffron.' She laughed, a sound like the clearing of pipes. 'The Alchymical wedding, in all its most lovely forms. Gold is for amateurs.' She turned her mechanical gaze upon Margaret. 'Now. You.'

Margaret shrugged. 'It's not –'

'Not working?'

'No.'

Lady Million raised herself from the seat, stalked over to Margaret, began to prod her here and there about the torso.

'You don't feel? Not a thing? Nothing penetrates?'

'Physical things.' Margaret shrugged again. 'Pain, cold, you know. Nothing emotional.'

'No laughter? Fear?' she snapped her fingers before Margaret's eyes, peered into her ear, up her nose. 'Love?'

'No.' Margaret gazed steadily out the window, at the bombsite of weeds and rubble beyond. 'No love.'

'And this is important?'

A rat peered at Margaret from the window of a rusted car, then withdrew into the dark. 'I don't know.'

'But you want to.'

'Still.'

Lady Million turned away, walked to the window, and stared at the sky.

'One hundred and sixty-five years, seven months, three days, twenty-one hours, several minutes, assorted seconds. A long time. Still you all come. Problems, problems, problems. No matter the country, or the time. You all come.'

'I'm sorry.'

'No.'

Margaret bit her lip. 'No. I guess not.'

'If you were, the problem would not exist.'

'No.'

Lady Million returned her gaze to the room. She clapped her hands, a sound like cymbals. 'Still. If you did not come, the solution would not be found. I have never failed. Never. Not with Kings, nor Fuehrers, nor Godmakers. In what do you work now?'

'Work? Um. I was in advertising, last time. I'm in web design now. Contract work.'

'A web designer. Not worth becoming my first failure. Not after Kings and ...' Lady Million waved her hand. 'And so on and so on. This time, this time, I will find what you need.'

'I don't even know what I want any more.'

'I don't care about want. Now sit.'

She indicated a chair in the darkest recess of the room, a complicated web of wires perched upon it like a crown. Margaret sat, wiggled her backside around until she was comfortable.

Lady Million threaded a long tube onto a hypodermic, swabbed a spot on Margaret's temple, and carefully inserted the needle into the skin. Margaret sucked air between her teeth. Previous experience kept her from flinching. Lady Million drew off several millilitres of milky fluid, and frowned.

'So little left. This will be the last time, old girl. The last time for us both. You are bereft of essence.'

'So soon?'

'So soon? Pish. Nobody bothers me as you do. You are quite drained, my girl. Drawn dry. This is the last time.'

She withdrew the needle and placed it to one side. Moving about the machine, she encased Margaret in the cage of wire. Countless tiny spikes pressed against her skin at head, face, throat and wrist, points nestling inside the healed over puncture wounds that littered her body.

'One more time to capture your dreams,' Lady Million said. 'One more time to bring them to life. Don't blink.' She clanked across the room to rest her hand atop a large, tape-wrapped lever set into the wall. 'This is going to hurt.'

Margaret stared at the world outside the window. With a sigh of expelled steam, Lady Million lowered the lever, and the world turned black.


*Rubedo*

The problem was, she could never have loved him, no matter how much she needed it. No matter how many bodies filled her bed, or whatever drugs, blades or fluids she used to batter her nerve endings, the core of her remained indifferent. Nothing reached inside. The void remained empty, pressing against her organs, deadening everything it touched. Nothing had changed, not in all the months since her visit to Lady Million. Not since then, and not in all the years before. It was not that the failures proved so disastrous. It was knowing the inevitability of failure, and still being compelled to try.

The taxi arrived, the lover departed, and a small interval of peace descended. Again, and again, and again.

Today, however, a change: the taxi was gone, and a courier van filled the driveway. A uniformed figure approached, knocked on the front door. Margaret signed the proffered form, received the brown-wrapped package. A flat box, perhaps four inches thick, long and wide enough that she chose to lean it against the arm of her sofa rather than attempt to lift it onto the coffee table. She curled her fingers over the top flap and pulled, revealing the contents in one long tear of cardboard.

A mirror, simply framed, reflective surface gleaming a dull brass in the light from the single lamp. A small sheet of something like thick paper was taped to its surface. Margaret fingered it. A spark of something tickled her inside. The sheet was not paper, but vellum- smooth and supple beneath her fingers, slick as she pulled it from its mooring. She recognised Lady Million's rounded, feminine hand in the letters stained into its surface. She read.

> Dear Madam,
> A surprise. Not what you expected. There was so little of you left. So few drops of essence. Not enough to transmute blood or dreams. Enough to spread over a surface. Enough, I hope, to show you. What? Who knows? A mirror made of you, dear Margaret. Let it not fail.
> M o'C

Margaret ran a finger over the mirror's surface, frowning. It was soft and warm, sticky, not at all the cold, smooth metal she had expected. In the mirror, her doppelganger frowned and removed its finger from the glass. Margaret bent, and peered closely. The image was dark, its outline vague and wavering. She stood and recovered the lamp from the far corner of the room, set it upon the coffee table, and knelt before the mirror again. The light worked- she saw herself, the details of the room stark behind her. Still, the image bore soft edges, almost out of focus, as if a million tiny imperfections caught the light and diffused it. A fault of the odd surface, Margaret decided. A flaw in her essence.

There was something else wrong with the image, something she could not quite put her finger on. Margaret traced her outline. There she was, in the centre of the glass, in her shirt and trousers, and with a look on her face that countless men had referred to as the final straw. The lamp was there, casting its light. The coffee table, the curtains ... there. Behind her, to the right. A figure. A dim smudge where she should be able to see to the wall. As Margaret watched it came closer, became clearer. A man. There was a man. Margaret spun away from the mirror with a gasp, then stopped short. The room was empty. The coffee table, the lamp, the curtains. Nothing else. She turned again to the glass. He was there, almost touching her shoulder. Margaret reached out behind her, felt nothing.

'What the hell?'

There was more, now, Margaret saw. A fault with the man, something wrong, or missing. He was beautiful, breathtakingly so: short without appearing small; lean; his chest the perfect size to balance his hips; elfin features atop a long neck; suntanned skin the colour of lightly burnished bronze; short hair curled around delicate ears. His almond eyes met hers. He smiled, and in that smile lay all the joys that had avoided her for as long as she could remember. Margaret gasped. A bolt of heat struck the centre of her chest, tearing her breath away. The man stepped in front of the mirror-Margaret and raised his hand. He was perfect, as perfect as any desire she could ever have. And exposed to her gaze as he was, with nothing between them but the surface of the mirror, the light from two lamps playing across his, front and back, Margaret saw the wrongness she had been unable to place. His skin was not just the colour of bronze. It was bronze.

The man in the mirror was made of bronze.

They stayed that way for several minutes, staring at each other across a gulf of space and understanding. Then, with a smile so sweet it made the void inside Margaret ache, he raised one perfectly forged hand, and beckoned her: closer, closer. Margaret fell to both knees, inches from the mirror. Without knowing why, she raised her hand and pressed it against the sticky surface, like a prison inmate in an interview booth, desperate for the touch of a visiting lover. The surface resisted her briefly, then her hand sank into it, deeper than the millimetres-thick plane. She let go a shout of surprise. On the other side of the image, her hand appeared. Only it was not her hand but a simulacrum, in every detail a perfect imitation of her own, forged from glinting bronze.

Margaret wiggled her fingers, and the bronze hand in the mirror did the same. She clenched her fist, and watched the metal fingers curl over until they pressed against their palm. She pulled back, and her arm came out of the glass. The hand slid backwards until the heel was on one side and the fingers were on the other. Margaret stared at it, then leaned forward again.

'How? I don't...' But of course, she did know. It was Lady Million, and her essence, and the need that had been drawn out of her – transformed, transfigured, given shape. She looked into the perfect eyes of the bronze man. He reached out, and his hand nestled inside hers.

And suddenly, just like that, the barrier that surrounded her void was ruptured, and into the breach poured ... she didn't know, didn't have the words, but it was hot as blood, and it stung, and the emptiness inside her drank and drank and she was crying and laughing and so... so...

'Oh, oh, God. Oh, God.' She brought her free hand to her face, and wept into it. 'Oh, God.'

And slowly, slowly, the first, boiling rush of emotion thickened, settled, until the void was full and only gentle waves lapped at the edges. Margaret raised her head, drew the back of her hand across her face, tears and snot mingling in a long streak. She sniffed, brought her breathing under control.

'Oh, God,' she said to the man behind the mirror. 'Is this what it feels like? Oh, God. Do I love you?'

He smiled, and pulled on her hand, drawing her closer to the surface of the glass. Margaret resisted, looked around- at the room, the furnishings, the fixtures. Nothing here, she realised, nothing that isn't beyond the mirror. Nothing that isn't replicated. She turned her gaze back to the glass, and the one thing she could not find anywhere else.

'But what if... ?'

She paused. What if what? She looked at herself in the mirror. What happens to her, she thought, if I'm there too? Does she disappear? Do I? And if I disappear, will anyone notice? Will they care?

And she realised: it doesn't matter. None of it does. Whatever happened, she would not be alone. Whatever happened, he would be beside her, and if not him, then someone, and she would love him.

She would love him. And for that small fact, that one small fact, she would risk the answer to any question.

Smiling, crying, happy, Margaret bent forward and leaned beyond the mirror.

# Beowulf in Brisbane
## Philip Neilsen

Twenty students sat chatting in small groups on the blinding blue carpet outside the tutorial room. What snippets he heard of their stories suggested small injustices or joys. They took up backpacks and followed him in, to chairs anchored in a semi-circle. The council of wisdom, as he had called it in a whimsical moment of the first week. The Great Books class was diverse – ranging from creative writing students to pilgrims from law and information technology. The idea of reading eight book-length classics was exotic to students reared on a school diet mainly composed of fragments.

> 'Reading these books will help you understand others better
> – to live in their shoes for a while. And it will tell you things
> about yourself too.'

He'd said that in the very first lecture – and he believed it. Two hundred faces had looked back at him with scepticism. Many promises had been made to them. They wanted proof. That was only fair. It was a congregation without a binding faith.

He had read from his lecture notes: 'In this subject, just like the warrior Beowulf, you will wrestle with monsters in the form of very long novels and slay dragons by unlocking their secrets. Your warrior's reward and gold will be the pleasure and insights to be found in the world's best writing. And at the end of semester you will be able to say, as Beowulf does:

> We willingly undertook this test of courage,
> Risked a match with the might of the stranger,
> and performed it all.'

They looked intently at him. It had sounded uplifting when he was writing the lecture at 1:00am. But at least a few were smiling.

> 'And of course, being a better reader will make you a better
> writer.'

They had probably heard that one before too. And he repeated the analogy of how you can't just sit down at a piano and expect to start playing Mozart or jazz. The words went out into the large lecture theatre and fluttered to the ground, perhaps to rest on a shoulder here and there, like dandruff. He wondered if anyone had dandruff these days. It was unlikely. What was certain was that even in a digital age the motivating dream of most creative writing students was to see their name on a book in a bookstore. Precious few would.

The text today was *Wuthering Heights*. The lecture before the tutorial had been going well – the Kate Bush music video (they liked the music, laughed at the choreography – he pointed out that she was sending herself up – a genius at nineteen), the PowerPoint images of the moors and Haworth, the Romantically suitable short lives of the four siblings, the return of Heathcliff as avenging entrepreneur in shiny boots to take over the Grange. Then, while mentioning the overlap of Gothic novels and vampire movies he had made an off the cuff joke about crosses:

'It's amazing how ferocious vampires, capable of acquiring enormous amounts of castle real estate in a very competitive castle market – not to mention being immortal and having superhuman strength and intelligence – are supposed to run away whimpering when confronted with two bits of wood stuck together.'

Generous laughter for a slightly laboured joke. But the promising mood of the lecture hall was shattered by a thin young man of about 25 in a white shirt and dark tie. He stood up and shouted:

'Stop laughing! This is blasphemous!'

Complete silence. Oh shit. The man pointed at him.

'You shouldn't make jokes about things that are evil.'

The automatic response after years of experience was to go into conciliation mode:

'I agree with you. But I'm sure no one here was mocking religion – I certainly didn't mean to. We were laughing at superstition.'

The young man stood there rigid with intensity for a few more seconds. Then he grabbed his knapsack and walked quickly up the steps and out of the theatre.

A murmur started and began to build.

'Okay – okay now – back to the lecture. Emily Bronte uses elements of the Gothic genre – to create atmosphere, for example – but *Wuthering Heights* is not a Gothic novel.' He heard himself saying this. The sterile light of the lecture room flashed with images – Emily standing in the rain at Branwell's funeral, Cathy's bleeding wrists, the young man's trembling anger. He and the class conspired to ignore them.

'That was a dramatic lecture,' he said with forced levity to the tutorial. Sympathetic chuckles.

'There's lots of fundos on campus,' a laidback boy with long hair said.

'Yes – there are,' he answered, grateful for this small solidarity. 'But universities are about questioning your beliefs. I've had a student refuse to read a novel because it has pre-marital sex in it.'

More chuckles – but also some wariness.

'What did you do?' asked the laidback boy.

'Well, look – I met Bishop Spong once and asked him what I should do when students refuse to read books on religious grounds. I guess some of you have heard of Spong – he's a progressive American theologian – his books are best sellers. I thought Spong would say something like "you have to respect their views" – but he said "tell them not to be intellectually lazy". I thought that was a good answer'.

'Is that what you told the pre-marital sex student?' asked a girl at the back.

'More or less. Anyway – how many of you enjoyed reading *Wuthering Heights*?'

Almost all hands went up.

'That's great! It's not an easy read – but it gets you involved doesn't it?'

Nodding – sounds of strong agreement.

'I thought it really sucked.' A girl near the front had spoken with quiet but clear vehemence. A girl who always looked unhappy in these tutorials – who until today had said nothing, for all his coaxing.

'I'm interested to hear that, Belinda. Thanks for being honest. What was your main criticism of it?'

Belinda stared at him. Then she stared at the Penguin Classic that sucked. It lay insolently in front of her. Clearly it managed to rekindle the original animosity that had propelled her into expressing an opinion. Her face was flushed.

'I just, like, hated Cathy. She was just so – selfish!' She glared at him defiantly. 'They were *both* so selfish.' She looked down at the book again.

Had she experienced the consequence of another's selfishness – the offered heart broken? Had a clumsy mini-Heathcliff crossed her path?

'Okay – fair enough. But remember we talked about not discussing the characters as if they were real people – and about not making moral judgements on them. And we agreed to say more than whether we liked them or not.'

She glared at him. He turned and addressed the class.

'Did any of you find the novel made you think about how Romantic love is obsessive and destructive of people? Or did you think it represented love as transcendent of social norms and taboos? Or both.'

'I think the novel doesn't want us to see everything as right or wrong,' said the girl at the back. 'I think it destabilises us trying to do that. It wants us to suspend judgement.'

Before he could compliment the student on this observation, Belinda spoke again.

'If their love thing is so like you said, obsessive and destructive, then that's the same as being selfish.'

The girl at the back answered her. 'But what about when Cathy says "I *am* Heathcliff". Wasn't that going beyond the selfish? Totally identifying with another person?'

Belinda made a sound of choked off rage. 'No – it wasn't! She just wanted everything – that's all she's saying. She wants everything her way and she's really *selfish*.'


The tutorial took a detour around the impasse, revived, discussion flowed, Belinda did not speak again. They did a writing exercise – a short passage of description where nature is wild and alien to Lynton, but using Australian landscape elements instead of Yorkshire ones. Several clever scenarios were read aloud to general acclaim. They mimicked the novel's language with gusto. Belinda did not volunteer to read her work, though he could see that she had written some lines. It looked like the long-haired boy, Michael, was about to read when the hour was up. An accountancy tutor, her students lined up neatly behind her, knocked on the door.

The Great Books class filed out into a world of judgement.

The path back to his office skirted the top of the hill. The sun had almost gone, and black branches of struggling trees laced the horizon. At this time of year a gusting wind tugged at the hedges. It sent an orange plastic chair scraping along the concrete. But not the sort of weather you could lose your soul in. Even winter here was benevolent. That made the moors seem less threatening – loosened their purchase on the imagination.

He checked his emails. Twelve more in the three hours he'd been wandering the moors with self-absorbed Cathy. Admin and student enquiries. An exhortation to all academic staff to encourage students to fill in the all-important on-line evaluation of teaching survey (upon whose scores lecturers depended for promotion). And a reminder that his examiner's report for a creative writing MA from another university was due. It was a competent enough novel and a bumbling exegesis, composed of half-digested and second-hand ideas. Planning for his own new novel was at a standstill. He was attempting historical fiction for the first time – the kind of novel he liked to read himself, as well as the kind that won awards. Something set in the past with big themes embroidered on the backdrop – and in the foreground two or three characters who had illicit sex, or witnessed a murder, or discovered a family secret – something likely to produce surprise and intimacy.

When you rubbed real life against literature the results were unpredictable. Sparks could leap up, or just a dull grinding. John Fowles saw a woman standing on a pier lashed by waves. The image haunted him. But all he could see with his own novel was a woman standing in a room in 1942, with a bundle of letters in her hand. There was something of fire there – but the street noise, the rumbling sullenness of trucks made her turn away from him.

It could be another false start, or it could be he needed to look at that room differently. Then again, he could blame it all on Bloom's 'anxiety of influence'. What was the point of writing if you weren't a Bronte or McEwan? Why add to the procession of dancing dogs, standing on their hind legs at book launches?

The MA novel wouldn't even make it that far. A stream of consciousness ramble about not very much on a single afternoon. Oh Virginia, if only your disciples had a fraction of your talent.

He opened the document where he had started writing the examiner's report. His last sentences had been: 'The candidate has been courageous in limiting his narrative point of view to a central character, Timothy, who is less than sympathetic from a reader's point of view. It is problematical that this character seems to have a very limited emotional and intellectual range – especially as he is presented in the novel as being an award-winning novelist himself. His minutely rendered self-reflexivity does become a little tedious at times. The metafictional strategies are competently handled, but metafiction is a well-worn path these days.'

He rubbed his eyes and turned from the screen. Outside it was dark – the distant city lights bright and serene. He could see car headlights moving in a golden thread across the bridge, finding their way home. And below, students made their way briskly to bus stops, or to car parks near the river. No monster, mother of Grendel, mouthed its blood-revenge beneath the murky water of the Brisbane River. No Heathcliff dug his sweetheart from her grave.

He typed one more sentence in the report.

'In a nutshell, the trouble with this novel is that Timothy is really, really selfish.'

It felt good – though he knew he would have to delete it later.

Next week he would make an extra effort to make Belinda feel more comfortable in the tutorial. If she reappeared, that is. And what about the fundamentalist. Next week they were doing *Beowulf*. He would have to refer to Christian ideas in that lecture. If the young man shouted again, he would retort: 'Since the Rapture is about to begin – and the four horsemen are going to gallop all over us – does it matter what we say in this lecture?'

'And it will tell you things about yourself too'. But only if you doubt enough.

The computer beeped as another email arrived:

*Hey Rob.*
*Thought I'd send you my writing exercise to cheer you up:*
*Cathy and Heathcliff went to a relationship counselor somewhere in*
*Australia. No desert or red dirt canyons, just the outer suburbs –*
*brick houses, almost touching each other. The counselor lit two*
*candles and gave them a glass of wine each to calm them down.*
*Heathcliff drank his in one big gulp and kept scowling. The*
*counselor said: 'You guys have a weird lifestyle. You need to get out*
*more. Escape from the Grange while you can – capitalism is bad for*
*you. Set realistic goals. Make some friends. Avoid big black dogs.'*
*Cathy said, 'Thank you, good sir. Do you accept Visa?'*
*Heathcliff laughed savagely and his candle blew out.*
*Cheers*
*Michael.*

The window drew him to its moving face. The lights kept streaming out of the city. The distant kin of Hrothgar, bearing battle-gold to the halls of the brave. Hardy brick-dwellers, thriving where the earth's breast was fair.

# Beowulf in Brisbane [Bus line of new rabBi Remix]
## Ashley Hauenschild

'That was a dramatic start,' he heard himself saying.

'Is that what you told the pre-sex marital student?' asked a girl at the back – sympathetic chuckles.

Belinda made a sound of choked off rage. 'No – it wasn't!'

The automatic response after years of experience was to go into conciliation mode: 'Well, look, I agree with you.'

Oh shit. Complete silence.

In a nutshell, the trouble with this exercise is that they have probably read it before – no uplifting analogy or laboured joke. It's just a stream of consciousness ramble about not very much on a single afternoon. Before you compliment the student on this observation, note that metafiction is a well-worn path these days. So we should wrestle with monsters in the form of very short novels and slay dragons by unlocking their secrets. To begin:

> Heathcliff dug his sweetheart from her grave. She glared at him. He could, like you said, make an extra effort to make Belinda feel more comfortable. But only if you doubt enough. Instead, Heathcliff laughed savagely. He opened the document where he had started writing, saw a woman standing on a pier lashed by waves.

Okay – okay now – back to the lecture.

'Reading these books will help you understand others better – to live in their shoes for a while. And it will tell you things about yourself too.'

He believed he'd said that in the very first lecture. And two hundred faces had looked back at him with scepticism. Many promises had been made to them. They wanted proof. It was a congregation without a binding faith – it was only that fair.

He had read from the lecture: 'And in this subject, just like the warrior Beowulf, you will long for your warrior's gold, pleasure, and insight. But the world's best writing will be the reward.'

They looked intently at him, as does Beowulf. Why add to the procession of dancing dogs, standing on their hind legs at book launches? In writing the lecture at 1.00am it had to be found – that good answer.

'And of course, being a better writer will make you a better reader.'

And he repeated how you can't just sit down at a piano and expect to be Mozart playing jazz. The words went out into the large lecture theatre and fluttered to the ground, perhaps to rest on a shoulder here and there like dandruff. He too wondered if anyone had dandruff these days. It was unlikely. In a digital age, what was certain was precious few would dream of their name on a book in a bookstore. To see at least a few of the most creative students smiling was motivating – even the writing was.

The text today was *Wuthering Heights*. The lecture before the tutorial had been going well – the Kate Bush music video (they liked the music, laughed at the choreography – he pointed out that she was sending herself a genius), the PowerPoint images of the moors and Haworth, the Romantically suitable lives of the four siblings, the return of Heathcliff as avenging entrepreneur in shiny boots to take over the Grange. Then, while mentioning the overlap of Gothic novels and vampire movies he had made an off the cuff joke about two bits of wood stuck together:

'Amazing how ferocious vampires sounded when we were 19, and capable of acquiring enormous amounts of castle real estate in a very competitive castle market – not to mention being immortal and having superhuman strength and intelligence.'

Students are supposed to run away whimpering when confronted with small injustices, but the promising mood of the lecture hall was shattered by generous laughter. A slightly thin young man of about 25 in a white shirt and dark tie stood up and shouted: 'Stop laughing! This is blasphemous!'

The Great Books pointed at him (twenty sat chatting in small groups on the blinding blue carpet outside the tutorial room) and called him a whimsical moment of wisdom ... but you shouldn't make jokes about things that are evil.

The young man stood there rigid with intensity for a few more seconds. Then he grabbed his knapsack and walked quickly up the steps and out of the theatre. I'm sure the man was mocking religion. He certainly didn't mean to, but no one here was laughing at exotic superstition.

A semester started and began to build.

'Emily Bronte uses elements of *Wuthering Heights* to create the Gothic genre. Gothic atmosphere, for example, is not a novel.' The light of the sterile lecture room flashed with images – Emily standing in the rain at Branwell's funeral, Cathy's bleeding wrists, the young man's trembling anger (he conspired to ignore them and the class).

The girl at the back said, 'Oh Virginia, if only your talent had a fraction of your disciples.'

It could be another false start, or it could be the distant city lights bright and serene.

The other girl at the back answered her. 'But what about when you rubbed real life against unpredictable literature? The results were sparks, John Fowles, an orange plastic chair scraping along the concrete.'

Nodding – sounds of strong agreement.

'Universities are about questioning your beliefs.'

'Yes – there are,' he answered, grateful for this small solidarity. 'But I've had a student refuse to have pre-marital sex.'

More chuckles – but also some wariness.

'What did you do?' asked a laidback boy with long hair.

'I met Bishop Spong and asked him what I do when students refuse joys on religious grounds. I guess some of you heard of Spong – he's a progressive American theologian – his books are best sellers. I thought Spong would say something like "you have to respect their views" – but he said "tell them not to". I thought that was intellectually lazy, more or less.'

'There's lots of fundos on campus,' the laidback boy said with forced levity to the tutorial. 'Anyway – how many of you enjoyed reading *Wuthering Heights*?'

Almost all hands went up.

He said, 'Great! What snippets of their diverse stories suggested a semi-circle?'

Murmur.

'I'm interested to hear from creative writing students ...'

They stared at him.

'I thought it really sucked.' A girl near the front had spoken with quiet but clear vehemence. A girl who always looked unhappy in these tutorials – who until today had said nothing, for all his coaxing.

He turned and addressed the class, 'It's not an easy read for students reared on a school diet mainly composed of fragments. Did any of you find the novel made you think about how love is romantic, obsessive, and destructive of people? Or did you think it represented social norms and taboos as transcendent of love? Or both.'

Belinda spoke again, 'I think the novel doesn't want us to see right or wrong as everything. It wants us to suspend judgement.'

'Okay – fair enough. But remember we talked about Belinda. What was the main criticism of her?'

Belinda stared insolently at the class.

'She read a novel clearly, because it managed to rekindle the original animosity that had propelled her into expressing an opinion.'

He had heard that one at his past tutorial ...

'That sucked,' he said, and gave them a glass of wine each to calm them down. 'Make some friends while you can.'

Her face was flushed. Had she experienced the consequence of another's selfishness? Had a clumsy mini-Heathcliff crossed her path? She glared at him defiantly.

The tutorial took a detour around the impasse, revived, discussion flowed. Belinda did not speak again. They did a writing – a short passage of description where nature is wild and alien to Lynton, but using Australian landscape elements. Several scenarios were read aloud to general clever acclaim. They mimicked the novel's gusto with language. Belinda did not volunteer to read her work, though she had written some heart broken lines.

When the sun had almost gone, and black branches of struggling trees laced the horizon, an accountancy tutor (her students lined up neatly behind her) knocked on the door: 'Thanks, but the hour is up.'

Cathy and Heathcliff went to a relationship counsellor somewhere in Brisbane. At this time of year a gusting wind tugged at the hedges – not the sort of weather you could lose your soul in. The path skirted Yorkshire, Hrothgar, Bronte, but the hardy brick-dwellers at last arrived.

The counsellor lit two candles. Heathcliff drank his in one big gulp (cheers) and kept scowling.

Cathy said, 'I think it destabilises us – trying to do that.'

See, in totally identifying with another person, books become self-absorbed, a little tedious. The MA novel wouldn't even make it that far. Could it be that characters love a world of judgement? Something more than whether we liked them or not? A reminder that real people, anchored to a selfish historical backdrop, could leap up and set realistic goals! The idea was benevolent, less threatening than academic staff and their fundamentalist cheer. An exhortation to characters who had illicit sex, or witnessed murder, or discovered a family secret – something likely to produce surprise and intimacy.

Thank you, and next?

Heathcliff hated Cathy. Cathy was just selfish.

The counsellor: 'You guys have a weird lifestyle. You need to get out more. Escape from the Grange – capitalism is bad for you. Avoid big black dogs.'


Beowulf rubbed his eyes and turned from the screen. Outside it was dark. He was attempting fiction for the first time – the kind of novel he liked to read himself, as well as the kind that won awards.

Or just dull grinding? The image haunted him. There was something of fire there – but the street noise, the rumbling sullenness of trucks, made courageous narrative just another point of view. He checked his emails, a bundle of letters composed of half-digested and second-hand ideas. But all he could see was his own moving face.

# Cherished

## Emily Maguire

This girl I hang out with sometimes wears shiny red polish which draws attention to her ragged nails and sunless skin. Silver bikie rings squat on her stumpy fingers.

Her eye-makeup is always uneven. This is not a fashion statement; she does not flaunt a retro-blue-frosted left eye and a goth-inspired-charcoaled right. It is only that she is easily distracted and so will forget to apply a second coat of mascara on one eye or blend the liner on the other. From a distance it looks fine, but up close the imbalance is off-putting.

Her hair is the colour of dried blood. It smells of chemicals and is stiff to the touch. In a photo taken on her sixteenth birthday it is waist length, shiny and brown. I asked her why she changed it but she only laughed.

When she dances or argues she grows a perspiration moustache. During sex, sweat coats her forehead even if the rest of her remains dry and cool.

A tan would disguise the steel-blue veins radiating from her areolae, but she is not the type to sunbathe topless nor is she a woman familiar with salon treatments. She leaves her disposable razors in my soap dish and her tweezers on the basin.

I think her gums are unhealthy, because one time she borrowed my toothbrush and left behind a smear of pinkish toothpaste at the base of the bristles.

I suggested she buy some new jeans after I overheard a mutual friend make an unflattering comment about the size of her arse, but her new jeans were even tighter. The angry lines they leave on her belly make me think of childbirth.

And yet when she checks her reflection in my bathroom mirror, she smiles like she has caught sight of a beloved friend.

# Cherished [Beloved Friend Remix]
## Michelle Almirón

A long time ago, I had waist-long hair; shiny and brown. After washing it, I would sit in the sun-room as my mother brushed with gentle, even strokes and slowly, the long healthy strands would dry naturally. As I walked around, the thick tresses acted in concert and moved like a ballerina's voile skirt.

Every morning, after putting on my school uniform in slow motion in front of the heater, I would sit at the kitchen table, tilt my head to the side, and slowly plait my hair with my stumpy fingers, then neatly affix clips to my head to take care of any flyaway strands. When I slouched on the chair, eating my breakfast, I could see the button-holes in the chest of my school dress strain open, like feral cat eyes changing into something ethereal.

As I got to school, I would sit at my desk at the back and hide behind gothic comics as other girls ran around the room, telling each other about who was hot, who they got on with and who was a slut. Sometimes, I took the time to quickly do homework, but that was only if I hadn't finished it during class the day before.

Every day, I sat in the far-off seats that circled the perimeter of the school, concealed from everybody, hoping somebody would veer off the territory of their social clique and start chatting to me. But they never did.

I decided to take matters into my own hands when a new girl came to school. I offered to show her around. We hung out for a couple of weeks, where I shared my comics with her and showed her my goth drawings. She said they were good.

I said – meet me next to the Drama Room – as I went off to another class. I sat on the cool grass under the tree, waiting. I started to nibble on my nails, biting the soft flesh, causing it to bleed a little. I would soothe it, lapping it with my tongue and savouring the tangy aftertaste of my own blood. After a while, I got up and went to the toilets, the hidden way I had devised so nobody could see me but I could see everyone. I heard my new friend talking to a group of girls in my year level. She said – she's so weird. Her drawings give me the creeps, you should see them. I swear, she's a freak! – they laughed.

That afternoon, I went home and stole twenty dollars from Mum's wallet. I went to Priceline and bought some hair colour. In my bedroom, I got my craft scissors and started to cut chunks of my hair off. Then, I followed the instructions and dyed it. As I looked at myself in the mirror, I promised myself not to wait for anyone to discover whatever it was that I wanted to share with the world. Instead, I would be my own beloved friend.

# Dara's Firebird Lovesong
## Damian McDonald

**PART ONE**

Dara and Jody sat on the sun-scorched concrete with their backs against the bus shelter. They were sharing an apple, one of those tart green ones, and as Dara took her turn gnashing into it, Jody gagged and vomited up some peel.

'Shit, are you okay?' Dara asked, rubbing Jody's back.

'Um, yeah,' Jody croaked, and started to laugh. 'Just dying of apple peel.'

Dara began to laugh too. Looking at the little pile of fruit skin and foam brought on more laughter, and they were both suddenly breathless but unable to cease the spasms of laughter hiccupping up from their stomachs. They had to lean on each other to save falling over, and even the tut-tut tongue-clicking of the old Italian lady having to divert around them on the footpath could barely stop the infinite but elusive humour. The bus droning into the stop enabled them some composure, but once on board just looking at each other was enough to start it up again.

This was the coolest day Dara had had in forever. Jody and her had decided to wag school just that morning before rollcall, and despite her anxiety – this was actually the first time Dara had ever wagged – she was so, so glad she did. They were both in Year 11, and had only become friends three months earlier. They were from totally different scenes at school, but one maths lesson had changed all that. Jody had borrowed someone's correction fluid – in fact it was Mr Dickinson, the teacher's correction fluid – but it was borrowed from someone who'd borrowed it from him. At the end of the lesson Jody was packing her stuff up and didn't know what to do with the bottle of white-out, so she tossed it out the window of the classroom. Dara had seen her do it, and thought it was just so cool. Jody had done it not in the hope of getting attention, because no one was paying attention, they were all packing up their own crap as fast as possible; she'd just done it. She looked at the bottle, didn't know what to do with it, didn't want it, so just casually tossed it out the open window behind her. Mr Dickinson began hollering for his correction fluid. Jessica, who Jody had borrowed it from, shouted that

44

Jody had it as she left the classroom. Jody pretended she didn't hear, Dara could tell, and zipped up her bag. Mr Dicko stopped her at the door though, and asked for his bottle.

'Um, I don't have it, sir,' she said.

'Well you're not leaving until I get it back,' he told her.

Mr Dicko was a complete wanker. Dara disliked him most out of all her teachers. He was just so humourless, and he always had tiny beads of sweat on his forehead; Dara imagined they must smell like the water from boiled pork bones. Stuff him, Dara thought.

'Here, I had it,' Dara said and retrieved her own white-out from her bag.

'Thank you, Dara. I know *you* pay attention in my class,' he said and raised his overgrown eyebrows at Jody.

Whatever that's supposed to mean, Dara thought.

Dara handed Dicko her white-out and Jody and her headed out for lunch.

'Thanks, um, Dara. Dicko's such a dick.'

'Yeah, he sure is.'

'You saved my arse there. That's very cool of you.'

'No worries,' Dara said.

Jody was one of the cool chicks in school. Always had been, since Year 7. Boys always liked her. Her natural blondeness, blue eyes but dark skin, conformed exactly to so many tastes. Jody was always effortlessly a part of all the cliques. Dara was geeky when she'd come to high school. She was thin, short, flat-chested, wore glasses, and her actual enjoyment of class-time put her at odds with the cool kids. But by Year 11 Dara didn't care so much about being cool and appealing to the masses of Marrickville High. She'd started taking guitar lessons in Year 9, and was getting pretty good. Music had become her life, and she'd become the school expert on everything rock n roll. She felt comfortable with herself, and even a little cool. Despite the geeky approach to her immense interest in rock music – studying everything she could get hold of about her favourite musos, and practising guitar at least four hours a day – it'd paid off. Her peers found her genuinely interesting. Becoming friends with Jody was an unexpected, but nonetheless cool coup though. Dara would be right at the top of the stupid social order when she moved into her final year of high school.

The girls walked into Steve's Guitars and Dara actually blushed when she saw it. It was like seeing a rock star hanging up there on the wall. A Gibson Firebird; and not a re-issue. Just like the one Dave Grohl from the Foo Fighters uses. Not one of the original daggy reverse body design ones, but a much cooler looking late 60s banjo tuners one. Black with a white scratch-plate. Just like Dave's. Dara was speechless. It was too high for her to reach, so she breathlessly asked Jody to get it down for her.

'What? This old one?' Jody said.

'P-please,' she whispered.

It was beautiful. Neck through body. Not too heavy. And signs of tough love all over it. She strummed it with the pick she always kept in her pocket. It was in tune. The action was so low it felt like she was playing cool air. Not like her old bomb of a Les Paul copy. She played some of her favourite songs, and it looked like Jody was getting bored, but Dara couldn't stop playing.

'You like the Firebird, hey?' Steve said.

'I'm in love,' Dara said.

'They're not for everyone. Give me an SG any day, but if you want it, I can let it go for fifteen hundred. I got a good deal on it.'

'Please, please don't sell it. I'll get it. I just need to, um, you know, convince my parents.'

'Tell you what. I'll tell people it's sold. For a few days.'

'Thank you. It's perfect.'

'If you say so.'


Dara couldn't believe the day she'd had. She'd jigged with Jody – who she was sure she was developing a massive crush on – and found the most absolutely awesome guitar. She felt like she was on the precipice of ultimately cool things happening to her. She'd already convinced her parents that she needed a new guitar. Hers was becoming embarrassing – constantly slipping out of tune and the pick-ups cutting out. Fifteen hundred was a lot, but her grandmother had left her and her sister three thousand each. She'd tell her parents she'd never ask for anything else. And she actually believed she never would. And as for Jody, who couldn't believe that she actually loved that old scratched up guitar, well, Dara would be happy if they just stayed friends, but if anything more should happen, she'd be more than happy. She could tell Jody liked her; it was just a matter of how much.

Dara's dad could be such a pain, but it was cute the way he was trying to get a better deal on the guitar.

'And what about the strings? They look old and will break I reckon. Don't you think you better throw a couple of packets in?'

'Ah, well, the strings were put on just a week ago, but sure, why not. I'll chuck in two packets of D'Addarios.'

'Good, good. And a lead? One comes with the guitar?'

'Dad!'

But getting the Firebird home and plugging into her little Marshall fifteen watt and playing everything she knew was, well, the term that came to mind was *better than sex*, though she'd never had that. And she felt if she could just have this guitar forever, she'd never need it. And that night she couldn't sleep for just laying there looking at the guitar on the stand at the end of her bed, perfect in silhouette.

The weekend her parents went to Dreamworld and Movieworld with her little sister, Dara invited Jody to stay over. Jody suggested having a party, but Dara said her parents would find out and shit. Really though, she just didn't want anyone else there. Dara did have other friends from school, but they were more like her: less into the social side of school, and way more into how what they did at school would shape their academic and professional careers. Dara felt almost one hundred percent sure she'd be accepted into conservatorium after Year 12, and so could afford to put a little time into the now of her life.

Jody turned up several hours after she said she would, but seemed in high spirits and had brought a bottle of sherry she'd knocked off from her mum's place. They had a few glasses of the booze, and Dara had never tasted anything so disgusting. Sweet at first, but then something like foul bile juice. Jody didn't seem to mind it at all. Dara played Jody some of her favourite CDs: Nirvana, Foo Fighters, The Strokes, The Beatles, Led Zeppelin, The Who, The Stones – all the cool guitar songs. They danced, and laughed, and talked about the other kids at school.

Jody had slept with some of the boys, and Dara was shocked to hear about how they acted with Jody; the boys seemed so confident and blasé at school, but from what Jody was saying, they were just like little kids – embarrassed about their penises and what they couldn't do with them. Jody asked which guys Dara liked. Dara picked randomly, because she didn't really like any of them. Not even just to talk to really.

'Brett Ellis is cute,' she said.

'Yeah, Brett's not bad. But he's going out with Meredith.'

'Oh,' Dara said, and hoped that conversation was over.

Jody asked to use some of her makeup. She didn't have much – just stuff people had given her as presents. They sat in front of her bedroom mirror and studied each other's faces.

'You're so lucky,' Jody said.

'Me? Look at you.'

'You look so good in black, Dara. You can just wear anything as long as it's black and you'll know that it suits you.'

'But you can wear anything. Anything at all, Jody.'

'Nah. For a start, I can't wear black.'

Dara had never seen Jody wear black, it was true.

'But anything else.'

'I wish I had your hair, your skin, your eyes. You don't even need any makeup.'

'You're crazy, Jody.'

'You're so lucky to be Asian,' Jody said.

Dara didn't know what she meant. And didn't really want to know. She did have Thai heritage, but it didn't define her. Not in her mind. She hated being reminded of it in that way: making it seem like such a big difference. She had so much more in common with Jody than with any of her cousins in Thailand. And it kind of hurt that Jody saw such a difference, whether she called being 'lucky' or not.

'Believe me, you're the lucky one.'

They made some Indian food, and just as they started eating, someone knocked at the front door. As Dara went to the door, she could hear whoever was there whispering. When she opened it, it was Peter Tootslakis, a Year 12 guy from her school. He must have been whispering to himself. Freak. She didn't know Peter at all – only that he was loud and had a large group of friends, mainly all the Greek guys.

'Yes?' she said.

'Dara, how ya goin', mate?' Peter said.

'Um, okay. What is it?'

'Just thought I'd come over, see what's happenin', ya know.'

'Oh. Not much. What do you want? I'm having my dinner.'

'Dinner huh? What are you havin'? Chinese or somethin'?'

'No.'

'So, what else is happenin'?'

'Nothing. Look, what do you want, Peter?'

'Just seein' how you are 'n' that.'

'I'm good. I have to go now,' Dara said. This was weird. This was just bizarre. What the hell was this guy doing here? She didn't know him. Had never, ever talked to him. And would never by choice. She didn't like the vulgar cockiness of Peter and some of his mates. They seemed to take pride in being ignorant.

'Hang on,' Peter said. 'So, do ya go to the gym 'n' that? Ya look pretty trim 'n' that. Like ya work out.'

'No, I don't.'

Dara heard someone whistle in the street behind Peter. It was one of those things he and his group did to each other at school – like using someone's name was beyond them.

'Okay, Dara mate. I gotta scoot now. You take care huh,' Peter laughed.

'Bye,' Dara said, and closed the door. Hard.

'Who was that?' Jody asked when Dara came back to the table. Dara was happy to see Jody hadn't continued eating while she was at the door.

'You won't believe it. Peter Tootslakis.'

'What did he want?'

'I have no idea. Did he know you were coming over here?'

'No, why? Is that what he said?'

'No. It's just that he's never talked to me at all. And I've never told him where I live.'

'Ah, don't worry about him. Let's finish dinner. Do you want another glass of sherry?'

'Yuck. No thanks.'


It was gone. Fucking gone. And the amp too. The Firebird, the case and the amp. Gone from her room. It couldn't be, and her mind wouldn't allow it either. They must have been moved. But her wide open window and curtain flapped with the flooding truth of it. Someone had come in through it and stolen her beautiful guitar.

'JODY, fuck, Jody. No.'

Jody came into the room and stood there.

'What? What happened?'

'My guitar. It's been stolen.'

'What? Are you sure? Maybe you put it away.'

'Just help me look.'

They began searching the house, Dara flushed with a hysterical false hope. And then it hit her.

'Jody. Jesus, that's why Peter Tootslakis came. Someone stole it while I was at the door. Did you hear them?'

'What? No, I didn't hear anything. I put that CD on.'

It was true. Dara hadn't even noticed. Jody had put on a Soundgarden album. Strange, she quickly thought, she wouldn't have picked *Badmotorfinger* as Jody's choice of record.

'Jesus Christ. I can't believe this. I'm calling the cops,' Dara said, pulling her hair back hard.

'The cops? Don't tell them I'm here.'

'Huh, oh, okay. Um, why?'

'Just, um, my brother's been in some shit with them. I don't want my name coming up with the cops, you know, my dad would crack a shit.'

'Okay. But I have to call them.'

'Yeah. I know.'


It had been three hours and the cops still hadn't shown up. Dara couldn't help it. She had to cry. Jody hugged her. Dara felt the comfort in it. And despite her loss, her chest flooded with the hot feeling of true friendship. She nuzzled Jody's neck. Jody rubbed her cheek on Dara's head. Then they kissed. Long, long slow kisses. Dara's head felt lighter than the oxygen around it. And she felt weak, but had the strength to kiss on like this forever. She could barely breathe, but felt she didn't need to. They kissed and hugged for what seemed like a very long time, but when the front door pounded she realised that she wanted it to go on for far longer.

Officer Polkinghorn seemed dubious. He asked where Dara's parents were at least eight times. And whether she was the only one home. Jody had gone into Dara's little sister's room and locked the door when the cop knocked so loudly at the door. Polkinghorn examined the window the guitar and amp had been taken out of. Then eventually said he'd pay a visit to this Peter Tootslakis.

Dara was wholly exhausted. After the cop left she fell onto her bed next to Jody and vanished into a thick sleep. Her phone was screaming at her to wake up some time later, and she had to reluctantly pry herself away from the warmth of Jody's arms and legs around her. Officer Polkinghorn informed her on the phone that Peter Tootslakis had been at home all night with his parents, and he was not in possession of her instruments. He then gave her an incident number for insurance purposes which she wrote on the back of her hand. Dara got back under the covers with Jody and her warm and sweet smelling body.


## PART TWO

Dara sat at her desk and thought back to the words Professor Lovelock had said at the beginning of her first semester at conservatorium. He'd asked the room of some two hundred students who of them were musicians. Everyone raised their hands. Then he'd asked how many of them were paid musicians. All bar a few dropped their hands. He then began asking students at random what they were going to do when they graduated. All were saying they would either become composers or professional musicians. Professor Lovelock then said that those who were already being paid to be musicians, maybe one third would be able to declare that their main income, and the rest of the room would become taxi drivers, sales assistants, administrative officers, telemarketers, waiters, and the luckier ones would become part-time function musicians or the really lucky ones music teachers. It was an ominous start to the degree, but Lovelock turned out to be a fun teacher and brilliant musician, and the degree was so cool that his words were forgotten, or at least repressed, along with the majority of things learnt in first year. But his words were true. Dara hadn't even ended up as one of the lucky ones. Well, nearly. She did work for one of the largest music act agents in the country. But she was an administration assistant. Everyone at the agency was a musician or an artist of some kind. The work wasn't so bad, and the people were cool, and she did get to meet most of the artists the agency represented. But some days it could be a bit depressing. And it made her think. What if she'd never lost the Firebird? Would her passion have stayed so strong that nothing could have stopped her becoming a successful musician? What if she'd just missed that lecture of Lovelock's, and his words weren't always at the back of her mind?

An incoming email notification on the computer screen brought her back. It was Andrew, wanting to know if she was able to meet for lunch. Andrew was a guy the agency often used as a sound engineer for newer artists. He said his talent was making drunk, sloppy musos sound slick and pro. It was true, Dara supposed. She'd gone out with him a couple of times, and he was nice, and didn't act cocky at all when it was just them, but she wasn't sure what she felt for him. She knew her parents would like him. He looked so young and clean. She felt that maybe she should give him a go. There wasn't much to dislike about him.

*Yep, where do you want to meet?* She replied.

They ate down at the Quay. It was a striking cerulean Spring day, and the sun on Dara's back was like a masseur's skilled hands. Andrew convinced her to have a glass of wine, and it only added to the perfect balance of weather and mood. Andrew was telling her about a band he was mixing and how he didn't think their career was sustainable, as they could barely play, and had to be wasted to do that. Dara had heard their demos and the first thing she'd noticed was that the guitarist's D string was way flat. They had a cool image though – not her thing, but certainly what was selling now – and, unfortunately, she could see that they would receive advances ahead of much more talented bands. Andrew was cute, but actually maybe a little conservative for her, Dara thought. Probably because of the wine, she could tell he really liked her. And he'd always agree with everything she said. And that was nice. But she felt she needed something more ... *dynamic* was the word that came to mind. But he did like her. And that meant a lot, didn't it?

They got up reluctantly to return to their jobs. Dara was a little dizzy. As they idled along the concourse, Andrew stopped her and kissed her on the mouth. She went with it. It felt like he'd thought about doing it for a long time, and was very anxious about it. But it was nice. He said he'd call her later, and looked like he had tears in his eyes. I must be drunk, she thought. She walked back to the office, relaxed, but not tired. A little wired actually.

She sat back at her desk and thought about the kiss. It was nice. It was nice that someone wanted her in that way. And it reminded her of a time. A beautiful, but also ugly time. The time she had with Jody back in high school. They'd kissed. And they were the most delicious kisses Dara had ever experienced. But they'd drifted apart not long after. Or Jody had drifted away. Jody had just started hanging around more with her people at school again. Even that arsehole Peter Tootslakis. And Jody knew exactly what he'd done. By the end of Year 12 Dara and Jody barely spoke at all. And Dara forgot about her. Or tried anyway. Jody would just appear in her thoughts. Like today. After kissing Andrew. Then Dara did something she couldn't believe she hadn't done before. A myspace search for Jody.

She hadn't changed much, from the photo she had up of herself. Location, Sydney. Single, orientation, bi. Dara clicked on *Send Message*.

> *Hey Jody, remember me? Must be what six years? Hope you're doing*
> *well. You look great. Would love to catch up if you're interested.*
> *Dara.*

She'd taken half an hour to write the two lines. Drafting and deleting. Finally going for the straight-to-the-point approach.


Three weeks. And Dara had noticed that Jody had logged into her myspace several times in that time. But finally, after almost a month she replied.

> *hi dara luv 2 catch up. i work at general pants in the city, near*
> *myer. come by and we'll hook up.*

Laugh lines were the only thing distinguishing the contemporary Jody from the high school Jody. Maybe her thighs were a tiny bit bigger, but that suited her. Dara was relieved that Jody seemed genuinely happy to see her.

'Oh my God! Look at you, Dara. So funky now. Very cool,' Jody shrieked when she recognised her.

'Hi, Jody. You look great.'

'Thanks. Look, I finish work at six. Why don't we meet up at the Art House and have a drink. I can't believe how funky you are now! So, six then?'

'Um, yeah. Six at the Art House.'

Dara thought it was a tiny bit rude of Jody to just dismiss her until after work so quickly like that, especially considering how far she'd had to walk on her lunch break. But she guessed Jody didn't know that. And it also proved that Jody really hadn't changed in six years at all.


'So I tried a bit of modelling, but could only get some bikini work and thousands of offers for nude modelling, but modelling's not my thing anyway. They kept telling me I'm too short. Too short, can you fucking believe it? So then I got a job in a call centre and saved up a bit and took a loan and went travelling across America, have you been? Mad over there. Anyway, then I met Roberto. Great looking, but knows it. And, as it turns out, an arsehole. He came back here with me, but only lasted three months. I bummed around staying at mum's for a while, but she wouldn't stop hassling me, so I ended up having to find a job. General Pants is my third and *last* retail job, I can fucking tell you. What about you?' Jody said, sipping her Vodka and lemon squash. Dara wondered how Jody could go from talking to drinking without a breath.

'Well, I went to uni, conservatorium of music, went to Thailand for four months, then came back and got the job at the agency. Not much else really. Still play guitar, but I never really got into a band or anything. Just record stuff for myself.'

'Ah. Still play the guitar, hey? So do you see anyone from school still?'

'Nah, not really,' Dara said, 'no one you would remember anyway.'

'Yeah, I didn't stay in touch either. Met too many cool people after school. Oh, no offence,' Jody added and took a long sip.

'I see. Yeah, I just concentrated on study. I know it sounds nerdy, but I was just glad when high school was over and I could try and start a whole new life.'

'I wish I went to uni,' Jody said.

'It's never too late.'

'Hey, I love this song!' Jody said, sculling down her drink. 'Let's have one more vodka and go dancing. I know a cool club on Oxford Street.'


The club stank of sweat and stale alcohol. It was half full and Jody seemed to know everyone. The music was way too loud, and all bottom end. And every song had the same composition: rudimentary three or four note keyboard melody played on the high octaves, bass line simply following an un-altering one-two percussion line with exaggerated bass and snare. After four more vodkas she felt as though she could dance to it though. But Jody would take off from the dance floor and run up to someone who'd just walked in, and Dara felt like an idiot left there alone. She sat in a booth and felt a little nauseous. She wasn't used to conveyor belt drinking. Two was usually her limit on a night out. After half an hour of sitting alone Jody brought some more drinks over. Dara had a sip but felt like she was going to puke.

'I think I'm going to go home, Jody.'

'Home? Already?'

'Yeah, I'm a bit too, um, tipsy. And I can see you have plenty of friends here.'

'Tipsy hey? That sounds interesting. Have another voddy and I might take advantage of you.'

Dara feigned a giggle and a smile.

'Look, I'm getting bored of this place. You wanna come back to mine for a bit?' Jody asked.

'Um, yeah, sure. Where do you live?'

'Ten minutes away. Just over in Surry Hills.'

'Okay. Let's go now though, Jody,' Dara had to leave. She couldn't take another minute in that foetid place.

Jody lived above a convenience store. The stairway up to it was very off-putting. It was narrow beyond belief, and Dara found herself wondering how in the world Jody got any of her belongings up to the flat. The precarious stairs also seemed to bow under Dara's slight weight. But inside the apartment Dara was relieved to find a quite clean and homely flat. Two small but comfy looking two-seaters sat nearly facing each other, not the TV, with a neat little table in between them. The window and surrounds were decorated with dark-red Indian inspired fabric, and most surprising was a wooden bookcase with two rows of books; the rest dedicated to CDs and DVDs. But still, Dara couldn't remember Jody ever reading a book at high school. Dara sat on one of the lounges and Jody bought them both a glass of red wine.

'It's just cask,' Jody said.

Dara wouldn't be able to taste the difference anyway. She sipped at it. It wasn't nauseating like the vodka.

'I can't believe how good you look now, Dara.'

'Thanks. You too.'

Toward the end of their night out Dara had started to regret hooking up with Jody again. But here, back in her flat – which smelled quite beautifully hinted with lavender too – she felt that attraction flooding back. The attraction she'd had for Jody as a teenager. It gave her a feeling she hadn't had since then as well: a feeling of hope and of something new and fresh – and just for her ...

'I'm starting to look old,' Jody said. 'But you've just gotten hotter.'

'You don't look ol—'

But Jody covered Dara's mouth with her own.


Dara had never had sex before. Not with anyone else anyway. And Jody had known exactly what to do. Everything felt so perfect it exploded out in almost endless crescendos. And Jody had looked so beautiful in the half-light of her little bedroom. Although Dara had thought about what she would like to do to Jody, she was a bit unsure when she actually had the chance. But when she started, Jody seemed to love what Dara did. Dara had been so into what they were doing all night she'd not even called or messaged her mum to let her know she wouldn't be home. Although she wanted to stay in bed with Jody forever, she knew she'd have to get up and call her mum.

It was early morning, but her mum would be awake. Her parents trusted her, but Dara knew they'd be worried as hell. Her mum was okay about it. She told her she'd stayed at a friend from school's place, and that she'd be home a bit later.

'A girl friend I hope, Dara,' her mum had said.

I hope she's my girlfriend, Dara thought.

She turned on the kettle and searched for a teabag. There wasn't much in the way of food and associated items in the place, but there was an ex-motel English breakfast sachet in the cupboard. She couldn't find sugar, but the tea was good anyway. Dara walked quietly around the flat. There was a small room next to the bedroom – too small to be called a second bedroom, but too big to be a closet really. She opened the door a bit and looked in. The homely order of the flat was counter-balanced in the room by stowed chaos. Things had been quite obviously pushed in there and the door shut. Half unpacked boxes, strewn clothes, piles of paper, even empty bottles. It was a bit of a thorn in the mood Dara had woken up in. It wasn't that bad really though. Jody had done a good job on the rest of the flat. And a wonderful job on her last night. Dara smiled to herself. She knew she'd have to take the dark with the light with Jody. She'd known that six years ago. Then something caught Dara's eye in the little room. A Gibson logo. Gibson? Jody hadn't mentioned having a guitar, let alone a Gibo. Dara put the cup down on the floor and ventured quietly into the room. She moved some boxes and clothes and cleared a path to the unmistakable emblem. It was a case. An old one. With quite a few dings. And one that was way too familiar. Adrenaline thumped into Dara's veins as she pulled the case out from under a pile of clothes and opened it up. Her Firebird. Definitely her Firebird. She took it out and turned it over. That wear mark on the back. Jesus. What the hell? Did Jody buy it somewhere? Did she buy it from Peter fucking Tootslakis? Dara instinctively held the guitar in the playing position, knocking a box off the top of something: her Marshall amp. There was an old toaster in the box and it hit the floorboards with a chunky metal-to-wood clang that hurt the silence of early morning. Jody pushed the door fully open, squinting, and showing now her age.

'What are you doing?' Jody groaned.

'What the hell, Jody. This is my guitar.'

'Oh.'

'How the heck did you get this?'

'Shit, Dara. It's too early. Come back to bed.'

'Come back to bed? How come you've got my guitar?'

'Do you want it? You can have it.'

'I can have it? Jody, please. What's it doing here? You don't know the shit I went through when this got stolen.'

'Look, Peter what's 'is name gave it to me.'

'Peter Tootslakis? I knew that arsehole took it! Jody, why didn't you tell me?'

'Because I asked him to steal it.'

'You? You asked him to?'

'Look, Dara, he was in love with me, so he reckoned. And he said he'd do anything for me. I wasn't interested in him though. I was interested in you. And I thought you liked me too. But when you got that guitar, all you loved, all you were bloody interested in was that thing. I actually hated seeing you play it. The look on your face. I asked Peter to knock it off.'

'Jesus, Jody. I did like you. And the guitar *is* a thing, not a person.'

'But you loved it like a person.'

'So if I had started being friends with another girl back then, you would have what, asked Peter Tootslakis to kill her?'

'Maybe.'

Dara put the Firebird back into its case, hauled the amp out from under Jody's crap and started dragging them both out of the room.

'Are you going then?' Jody asked, biting the nail of the right index finger.

'What do you think?'

'I think you're being cruel.'

'I'm starting to think I need to be cruel.'

The guitar felt the same as it had when she first played it, even though the strings were rusty as hell. Dara doubted Jody took it out of the case more than once. Her rage had given her the strength to lug the amp and the guitar out of the flat and into a taxi, but back at home her emotions were crashing in on one another like birds caked with oil slick. She plugged the Firebird in and started strumming. Chords and notes just came, fitting and flowing. Dara hummed a melody over them, and began turning it into words.

# Dara's Firebird Lovesong [Part Three Remix]
## Scott-Patrick Mitchell

These days, Dara's success was measured in sweat. There was the way it stung her fingers as they cusped on the edge of rawness. There was the way it stained her singlets, even if she wore them baggy and loose, billowing and braless. There was the way it licked its way down the crevice of her buttocks beneath her tight leather leggings. By the end of a gig it had ferociously lapped all over her, leaving her perfumed, soaked, exhausted. Yet elated. Wet with wonderment.

'Goodnight!' she screamed into the microphone, slacking her grip on the Firebird so it buoyed by her side, slacking like the sneer on her face.

She stalked off stage, the crowd whooping. She wasn't the only thing that was sweating in The OAF: everything was sweating, from Dara to the roadies to the other band members to the entire audience. Even the roof was sweating as the humidity in the low ceilinged club forced a precipitation of perspiration back on to the crowd. A steam, a frenzied haze of sex and song, music and mayhem, simmered up off the crowd and condensed in rivulets above them. The audience was baying for more, howling, clapping, cat-calling. They were a frenetic, adrenaline charged wall of fans and some diehard groupies, old skool riot grrls geared up with a dash of emo and grunge.

'Great show Phoenix,' her manager, Annie, called as Dara swaggered past her with the other Dentata girls. Her band mates chuckled and hollered, Sass high-fiving Dolly as all four of them strutted backstage to their dressing room.

Phoenix. The name brought a proud smirk to Dara's lips every time she heard it. The name was her *nom de plume*, her secret identity from the dreary, normal world she had left behind her. The world she only rarely haunted when, on occasions befitting her return, she'd try not to wear too much black to family events: birthdays, Christmas, Chinese New Year. Her parents had noticed the shift in her, the move from awkward to assertive, but had never really broached the subject. Or rather, Dara had never granted them the opportunity to broach the subject.

Elise, however, knew all about Phoenix and consequently the band, Dentata. Elise loved Phoenix. And quite unlike most promises little sisters promise to make – but invariably break – Elise had kept Phoenix a secret from their parents just as Dara has asked. Well, that's if you consider blackmail asking.

'You wouldn't!?' Elise had screamed the day Dara had sworn her to secrecy.

'Yeah, I will,' Dara had purred, cool and calm, confident behind her new persona. 'You see, it's simple Elise: you tell mum and dad about Phoenix and her band and I'll tell them about that trip to the doctor's we had to take when you were sixteen. Remember that? It was with Brett Ellis' little brother right? Gee, you wouldn't want to bring shame to the family name would you little sis'?'

'You mean like lesbian punk rocker Phoenix would ...?'

And from that point Elise had, surprisingly, kept Phoenix a secret. It was easy really: Phoenix was the big sister Elise had never had. Whereas Dara was dorky, gawky, awkward and shy, Phoenix was lean, mean, agile and keen – a wound up sex machine, part Agyness Deyn, part Lucy Liu. Whereas Dara would never say "boo", Phoenix would lead Elise by the hand into the darkest parts of the night, taunting the shadows and ghosts and ghouls to bring it, bring it on. Put simply, Phoenix was fun. Far more fun.

'Hey Sass,' Dara purred, 'come here and help me out of these.'

Backstage at The OAF, Dara lay on the couch and raised her long slender legs into the air, wiggling her bare feet, suggestively wriggling, her leather clad legs shiny and slick and long. Dolly laughed. Jess cackled. Sass walked over to Dara and with long slender arms, reached over the side of the couch and gripped Dara's hips. Her long porcelain fingers then dug in beneath the top of Dara's leggings and slowly peeled off the second layer of soaked skin. Dara exhaled languidly as musk enveloped the room. Sass lolled on her heels, her palms wet, her nose twitching.

'Oh Sass,' Jess snarled, 'you haven't a hope in hell.'

And with that she threw a towel at the back of Sass' head, knocking her from her fragrant daze. Sass blushed and threw the towel down at Dara, who giggled, kicking her legs at Sass so her black panties could be seen as her limbs gracefully nipped the air.

But it was true – for all the sex appeal, for all the constrained refrain that seeped from Dara when she was Phoenix, the one thing neither of them ever were was sluts. People suggested, yes. People even accused, passing a girlfriend's fancy and hero worship off as an outright affair. Dara had been confronted twice by psycho bitches, possessive lesbian groupies who believed their star struck lover was indeed doing far more than fantasising about being with Phoenix. And during both confrontations, Dara had laughed directly into the faces of the accusers, the one that had decided to wield a knife during the confrontation being punched in the face by Phoenix, suffering concussion, a broken nose, a small blackout and a whole lotta lost pride. And threats from the other members of Dentata, naturally. In fact, when Annie found out about the incident both the psycho girlfriend and moon-eyed lover – who had both been regulars at Dentata gigs – seemingly vanished and were never seen moshing again.

Dara never slept around. In fact, she had only had one girlfriend, but she had only lasted three months. She couldn't cope with the music. She couldn't cope with Phoenix. She couldn't cope with the self-confidence and containment that Phoenix had. Independence wasn't sexy to some people. So it'd been Phoenix who had broken off the relationship, not Dara. Phoenix wasn't about to see another girl come between her and her guitar.

Ah, the guitar. Patti. Named after Patti Smith. Such a nexus, such a dark star in the life of Dara. The return of the guitar, the reverse theft of it back into to her life just under two years ago had marked such a metamorphosis, such a flux in the life that Dara had lived. Songs had instantly seeped from Patti like tears for a long lost friend. Patti had been charged with such emotion, such pent up want to be heard that when Dara had begun playing her ... well, it'd been a matter of hours before the first song had scribbled itself down, a day later inked itself in. A week later and there were a dozen gems. Within a month and Dara was beginning to change. A confidence was burning from her cracked fingers, a swagger was in her step. Her body responded, as did her clothes, and a sexiness slowly engulfed every moment of her day like a star going supernova.

Andrew at the agency had tried to make an advance on her one day, near the photocopiers, after weeks of unreturned emails. Dara had calmly but firmly placed her index finger on his pouted lips.

'Andrew, no ... things are different now.'

'But I thought you liked me Dara,' he'd stammered, his pants clearly straining at the short high waisted skirts Dara had taken to wearing and the legs they now betrayed. 'We kissed. I thought it was a good kiss.'

'It was,' Dara cooed, 'but ...'

And she found it too awkward to tell him there so after work they went out to a rowdy bar Dara had chosen and she told him everything: about her childhood dreams, about the Firebird, about Jody and more importantly the return of all three of these things a month back. How now events had conspired to take her somewhere new, and she wasn't sure what was happening, or who she was becoming, but all she knew was that she liked it.

Andrew stubbornly understood, but when he later came back to her flat and listened to her play, his jaw dropped.

'Dara ... wow, I mean. That's so hot.'

'Thanks,' she blushed, but only slightly.

He leaned back on her tatty couch, 'You're so hot.'

What he had hoped to have been a purr came out a slur and Dara laughed.

'You're drunk Andrew. Time to say goodnight.'

Even though he had protested about being hustled into a taxi, the next morning he was at her desk, bleary eyed.

'Dara,' he winced, 'you play really good guitar. I mean, *really* good guitar.'

'Yeah?' she cooed, eyebrow cocked suggestively, white blouse unbuttoned to reveal the slightest of cleavage.

'Yeah ... listen, put together some stuff and come and see me in a few weeks. Professionally I mean.'

A couple of weeks later and Andrew introduced Dara to Annie, a new whiz he'd been training. Annie, all blonde hair and small figure, could've easily passed as a schoolgirl her features were that crisp and young. But the way she sized Dara up belayed a worldly charm. And when she heard Dara play, Annie's eyes blazed, and the schoolgirl she looked became something far more dark and inscrutable.

'Wow – she is good,' she said to Andrew before swinging back to Dara, 'but the name? The name doesn't gel. You don't seem a Dara – no offence – you seem something stronger, something unknown, something hereto unquantifiable.'

'How about Phoenix?' The name had been murmuring there at the back of her throat ever since Patti had come back into her life, ever since the Firebird had blazed alive again within her grip. And the name made sense, seemed to fit.

'I like it ... listen Dara – sorry, Phoenix – I've got some girls who are looking for someone like you. And you can sing. Damn you can sing. Dara, how would you like to join a band.'

Patti hummed, albeit only between Dara's fingers. Dara wasn't sure if she had struck the strings and believed she hadn't. It was as though Patti had answered for her.

'We'll think about it,' Dara said.

That night she played the Firebird until her fingers bled. She sang until her voice began to tear. She then put on old Hole records and danced and drank and gathered up all the bad memories of her life: school photographs, old tax returns, her work name badge. Out the back of her flat, in the overgrown garden she lumped everything into a large old flowerpot and set alight to everything within it.

'Come on then Phoenix,' she dared into the flames.

The dark curls of smoke snaked into Dara and there, beneath a harvest moon with a face full of fire and the smoke of a life spent, Dara felt Phoenix rise up, a light sweat beading across her lip, a slight sheen glistening her brow. Three days later and Dentata were signed.

Dara was drunk when she rounded the corner of her street. Drunk but excited. One hand was buried deep into the pocket of her designer cashmere trench coat, the other carried Patti in her case. Dara loved playing music. Loved the electricity it forged in her fingers, in her groin. She was drunk: on liquor and lyrics. But as she approached her flat she noticed someone out the front, loitering beneath the front lamp. As she got closer, she could make out the shape of a woman and for the first time in a long time Dara felt her insides constrict and twitch.

'My my my,' she snarled as she approached the blonde, 'look what the cat dragged in.'

'Dara!' Jody yelped, balling forward from her heels to toe excitedly. 'Or Phoenix, right? It's Phoenix now isn't it?!'

'Jody, what the fuck do you want?'

Dara dug deep into the pockets of her trench coat, balling up her fists. She hadn't seen Jody since the return of the Firebird, and now here she was, blonde and a little more washed out, yet still as seemingly firm beneath the tight sweater and even tighter jeans. Jody smiled softly, but when she noticed the nicety wasn't returned she kicked the toe of her boot and studied the motion before saying, 'Look, Dara ... fuck, I'm sorry hey. I'm really sorry for what I did.'

'Why are you here Jody?'

'To apologise!'

'You could've written a letter or sent flowers or, wait ... how about not even fucking bothering at all!' Dara snapped. 'Because you certainly haven't in the – oh – two years since I found out you were a lying thief!'

A taxi went zipping by. Across the street, above the town houses, Sydney glowed. Another taxi zipped by.

'Dara, I know I should've ... Dara, I'm sorry. I'm really sorry. I ...'

'Why are you here, really?!'

'I wanted to see if the rumours were true,' Jody stammered. 'I wanted to see if the same Dara I had a crush on in high school had grown up to become Phoenix, the hottest lead singer of the hottest all girl punk grunge band in town. And,' she paused, eyeing Dara up and down, 'the rumours are true.'

Another taxi zipped by. There was a humidity in the air, a heavy moistness.

'So you thought you'd come and get a piece did you?'

'Ha!' Jody threw her head back, the blonde hair catching the light, dazzling slightly. 'Me get a piece of Phoenix? Never. I came to apologise. That was all. Nothing more. Look, Dara ... what I did I did out of jealousy. I was stupid and young. Hell, I'm still stupid. I ... just want you to know I'm sorry for what I did. I wanted you, but didn't know how to get you.'

'You didn't need to get me,' Dara laughed. 'You could've had me – however you wanted me. I was mad for you Jody. Mad!'

'I know. Look ... Dara, I'm sorry. Good luck. You seem to be living it. Good bye.'

She smiled politely then turned and walked off, her shoulders slumped, her head down.

Dara fished out her keys, opened the front door, placed Patti inside and paused. She turned swiftly.

'Jody! Wait!'

Jody stopped and turned, a small smile on her lips.

'I shouldn't be such a bitch. Look, I'm not sure I understand why you did it, but I accept the apology. Look, would you like to come inside and talk about it ... maybe have a drink.'

'You sure?'

'Yeah ... but if I catch you stealing anything else I'll cut your fucking hands off.'

They laughed and Jody walked toward her, smiled as she crossed over the step into Dara's house. Phoenix closed the door behind them, watched the way Jody's firm butt clung to the inside of her jeans, wiggled in just that right way up the hall. *If payback is a bitch*, Phoenix thought to herself, locking the door, *then I'm just the girl to collect debts.*

# Take Away [daras-firebird-remix-lovesong]
## Tessa Toumbourou

Jody had driven across the city that day with the doors on child-lock so the woman in the back seat couldn't run out into traffic like she threatened, testing the door handle at each red light to press her point. She drove – lips pursed in a red-slash and deep furrow brows mirrored by the woman in the rear-view – to an address someone on the phone had suggested took people with these conditions. The voice was patronising and clinical, using the third person in a suggestive tone as if Jody might be asking for herself.

Driving home, alone, Jody passed the bus stop where years ago she and her old school friend Dara had once laughed so hard they couldn't breathe. Hysterical laughter, the kind that spasms from the stomach and leaves one breathless, the kind that even looking at each other had them exploding all over again. Life had been so simple and uncomplicated back then. Love was simple too – if you like someone you take something from them and hope they will see you clearer, hope that you can fill the spot that it took up in their lives. So simple she had asked Peter Tootslakis, the poor loser from high school who had liked her so much like a dog he'd done exactly what she asked him to do, to steal Dara's guitar. Yet, since then, she had felt so guilty she could never really face Dara again and their friendship slowly disappeared. Jody let her slip from her life, and everything else that was good with it. Having Peter steal that guitar for her was something she now regrets more than she could have ever imagined. It symbolises everything corrupt in her life, slipping out of her control.

It was over six months ago now that Dara had found the guitar in Jody's spare room in her flat, and had left again almost as abruptly, guitar in hand. In a terrible way it was an enormous relief to have been found out, to have the damn thing gone. The next day Jody had sent her an apologetic email on myspace, just two lines.

> dara, i'm really sorry i did that to you. it was a long time ago in my
> life. please don't hate me for something that happened so long ago. i
> want to change.

Dara wrote back a month later, almost to the date. To prove a point. Jody got it, loud and clear. You get what you give.

*Hey Jody, I'm not really sure what to say to you. I can take the light with the dark with you but that was just fucked up. I'm playing a show next Saturday at the Annandale. If your keen to chat, come see me there.*

Jody had shown up at Dara's gig, drunk and nervous, and the conversation lagged as Jody's eyes wandered around the room. Jody couldn't fix on Dara's face long enough to finish her sentences. Dara asked her to wait while she packed up her gear and loaded the car with the rest of the band. When she came back Jody had gone. Well, fuck you then, Dara thought, and left it at that.

Now, months later, all Jody could think about was how much she wanted to see Dara. More than want; she had no one else. She found Dara's number that afternoon, written on a piece of paper she still had from six months ago when they last met up, when Dara had come to find her at work and they had gone out drinking. The night sobered suddenly the next morning. Now or never she told herself, dialling Dara's number with shaking hands.

'I'm sorry to call you, are you busy?' Jody spoke too fast, her words spilling out incomprehensibly.

'I'm at work. Who is this?' But even as it left her mouth, Dara knew. Jody. Always so blunt on the phone.

'I didn't know who else to call. Can you come around? I'm at my mum's, a lot of shit has just gone down and I don't really know what to do.' Jody's voice broke down before she could finish her sentence. She sounded exhausted, and in a strange, sad way more genuinely Jody than Dara could remember in a long time. Dara's heart leapt.

'I just feel ... at a loose end.' My mother, Jody wanted to say, I'm turning into my mother. Hearing the urgency in Jody's voice Dara was compelled to say yes, of course, she would be there as soon as work finished.

Jody looked as exhausted as she had sounded on the phone. Her eyes, once animated and daring, were now bleary and red with dark rings underneath. Her blonde hair was tied back roughly in a ponytail. She seemed thinner than Dara remembered, even wearing a loose cardigan over her jeans it startled Dara to see how slight her body was, hardly needing to move in the doorframe to make way for Dara to let herself in. The house smelt faintly of lavender, and the cream coloured curtains were drawn even though it was still light outside.

Dara hadn't stopped at home to get changed and was grateful now as she stepped into Jody's family's home. She hoped her office heels and skirt gave a sense of efficacy – clean lines in a chaos world where children protect their parents from the destructive things in life. Dara knew, or had at least guessed, having seen the piles of dishes in the sink and put the pieces together, even before Jody explained. Her mother, newly separated from her second marriage, had taken to drinking. The past few months had culminated in the day Jody had come to visit her mother to find her passed out drunk on the kitchen floor, bleeding from the head.

'She could have died. And, when I got her up and took her to the hospital she didn't even care. She just came home and went right back to drinking.' She paused, looking up at Dara with eyes filled with fear, then continued. 'If she keeps this up she'll kill herself.' Jody stared down at the centre of the table blankly as she spoke. Dara sucked her breath in sharply at the thought of it, not sure what to say.

Jody explained that she had moved back to her family home since that incident, to keep an eye on her mother, but it hadn't made any difference. If anything it made things worse. 'This morning I found mum passed out again, the final straw, so I took her to an emergency rehab clinic some phone help line told me about.' Jody shivered, and then looked around her, noticing her surroundings for the first time since she had started speaking. She stood up and filled the kettle to boil water, fussing around in the kitchen to find tea bags. There was one left, an ex-motel English breakfast sachet in the nearly bare cupboards.

'But there's no milk or sugar.' Jody held the fridge open to prove it; the shelves held only a few ageing vegetables and condiments. Jodie laughed uncomfortably, apologising with a shrug. 'No one's been shopping for a while. I eat out a lot.'

'Black is fine. Hey, I remember that motel tea-bag brand from when I stayed at your apartment that time.'

'Yeah? Want to know why? My step-dad, the fuckhead, he stays at hotels and brings the toothbrushes and shit home. He told us it was for work. Turns out he was sleeping with his secretary. Bitch.'

'Shit, that's awful Jody. I'm sorry to hear that.'

'Don't be sorry. I'm sorry. That I'm a lying piece of shit like everything else in my life. That I stole your guitar to get your attention and never even talked to you after that. I can't believe you would come over now, after all that. No one else would.'

Dara stood up, her chair scraping loudly in the quiet kitchen, and went over to where Jody stood to hug her tightly. Apology accepted.

'It doesn't matter anymore. I've moved on with my life, things are working out with me.' Dara told her, breathing Jody in. Jody was warm and smelt sweet, the same slender body she remembered from the one intimate time they had shared, all stolen kisses and warm hands on soft skin. Jody trembled in her arms and almost immediately she began to cry, huge gulping sobs that seemed to come from deep inside her. She crumpled at the knees and, when Dara couldn't hold her full weight, they sank together to the kitchen floor where they sat, holding each other as Jody pressed her face against Dara's neck, her warm tears running in a shiver down her chest. Along with the deep sympathy of friendship, Dara felt flooding back the teenage attraction she had for Jody. She felt the faintest feeling of hope – perhaps something new could come out of all of this. She hoped that she could make Jody feel the same, to take the edge off her sadness. She stroked Jody's hair until her sobs eventually subsided. Finally, exhausted, Jody whispered to Dara that she needed to sleep. It was now completely dark and they had to feel their way out of the kitchen, along the hallway to Jody's bedroom. Neither bothered to turn on the light, it somehow felt easier to keep things in the dark.

'Can I cook you some dinner? You probably haven't eaten all day. I can just go down to the supermarket, or we could order some Indian takeout,' Dara offered, wanting to make herself useful, to be a comfort. Jody shook her head.

'No, please don't go anywhere. I'm not hungry. I just want to sleep. I haven't slept in months. Every night I lie awake to listen out for what my mother might do to herself. Now I know she's safe I can sleep. Anyway, I have to leave for work early in the morning.'

Jody had learnt the habit of drink before bed, keeping a half-empty bottle of whiskey by her bed. She shrugged when Dara asked her about it, said she needed it to sleep. She mumbled in protest when Dara took the bottle away but gave in on the promise that Dara would stay with her until she fell asleep.

Perfunctorily, like a nurse, Dara helped Jody wearily take off her cardigan and jeans. My role is a comforter, she told herself, as Jody lay in only her underwear, silhouetted by the street lamps that striped in bars of light across her face. She looked so beautiful Dara's throat caught. Jody reached up to kiss Dara hard, urgently unbuttoning Dara's shirt. Dara kissed Jody back on her tear stained face and neck, salty and sweet. Dara fell into bed beside Jody who turned over to tuck herself in against Dara and then fell slack, asleep in almost an instant.

Dara lay still to be sure not to wake Jody, trying to fall asleep herself. But sleep wouldn't come as she lay burning with the heat of desire while the girl she had wanted for so long, and had tried so hard to forget, slept pressed against her side. She imagined waking Jody with kisses, starting from her perfect feet, but waking her up would be selfish, and that was, evidently, not why she was here. Even the house itself seemed restless, shuddering into itself to match Jody's rough breathing.

In the early hours of the morning a noise in the front room made Dara sit up straight in bed and pull herself out of the covers where she was tangled up in Jody's arms and legs, and go out into the hall to see. Whoever it was had switched on the living room lamp, and she blinked as her eyes adjusted to the light. Jack, Jody's younger brother who she had met only a couple of times many years ago, was home from his takeaway delivery shift. He had the same heavy bags as Jody did under his blue eyes and his young beard was unshaven which suited him in a rugged, handsome way she rarely noticed in men. Perhaps, she thought, because he looked a little like Jody.

'Is that Dara? Jody took her time in luring you back.' Jack stood yawning, rubbing the back of his head, smiling slyly.

'We're just friends. She asked me to come over.' Dara spoke sharply, spun-out that Jack remembered who she was let alone her teenage love affair with Jody.

'Sorry, did I wake you?' He responded to her tone.

'No, I can't sleep.'

'Must be contagious. It's why I work so late – better than lying awake all night. I reckon it's this house that does it to you.' His voice finished with a question mark – but he seemed to be asking something else entirely.

'Jody asked me to come over. She took your mother to a clinic today, or yesterday rather.'

He nodded gravely – it had been on the cards. He hung up his jacket and went into his mother's room to find the bottles she kept hidden and then emptied them into the bath. The alcohol slapped against the porcelain, echoing with a vulgar sound against the bare walls.

He crashed around in the kitchen to make a cup of the herbal tea he had brought home, a sleep inducer. Dara didn't want it, the smell was strong and she knew why she couldn't sleep, but she sipped anyway to have something to do while he made polite conversation. He seemed to want to prove his family weren't all like that. Dysfunctional. Everyone has their own defence system – their individual coping mechanisms.

'Sorry you had to be here for this. It's really not your problem.' He rolled his eyes towards his sleeping sister's door, blaming her for inviting others to poke into their lives. He seemed much older than his 18 years, teetering now on the edge of adulthood with his heavy-shouldered responsibilities. Dara asked questions in the pauses but ran out of things to say before her tea was cold.

'Don't feel like you have to keep me company. You should just go to bed if you want to, you must be tired,' she told him. What was meant to be polite sounded halting and rude. She had caught him off guard. He shrugged and excused himself to bed to evade confusion.

*Bloody hell. Just trying to be polite*, Jody imagined him thinking.

Jody left early the next morning for her work shift. Dara woke up as she closed the front door on the way out and then couldn't get back to sleep – her mouth was dry and tasted of metal. The herbal tea must have worked because she had fallen asleep on the couch after Jack had gone to bed. She dressed quickly and boiled the kettle for tea. The sink seemed to be piled with every dish in the house; there were no clean cups left. She filled the sink to soak the dishes – to be useful, to create some order, to not have to think. Sunlight caught the empty bottles Jack had left on the windowsill, casting thin beams of light, which bounced off the white walls. She hummed quietly and focused on one dish at a time, washing twice to clean the congealed food that must have sat for some time. A key in the front door startled her from her thoughts. The door swung open revealing Jody's mother standing in the doorway, home to find Dara at her place at the sink. She was swaying slightly, keys in one hand and shoes in the other as though she was home from a nightclub or a party. Dara wondered how she had got here. Taxi? But the street was empty behind her and she carried no bag or purse. She pulled herself from her thoughts to greet Jody's mother.

'Hello, Helen.' Soap ran down Dara's arms and dripped off her elbows.

'Hello – Dara, is it? Jody's girlfriend from school. Doing our dishes. How presumptuous,' Helen muttered, as much to herself as to Dara, and pressed her lips into a smile but her eyes registered no emotion. Dara shrugged, bewildered.

'I used some for tea so I figured I'd do them all.' She stammered. The kitchen clock, she just noticed, read 10 to 8. With relief she realised she had to go, immediately.

'I should get going to work. Jody is at her work, at her General Pants shift.' Dara excused herself and let herself out the backdoor, face flushed. Jody's girlfriend from school, is that what she had been? Jody's family had even known and she hadn't? She felt she had somehow caught Jody exposed, slipped into the vulnerable interior of a life that seemed so tough on the outside.

Jody called later that day to tell Dara that her mother had left 10 minutes after she had arrived at the rehab centre and had walked home. It had taken her all night.

'I can't do this much more,' she sighed. 'So I'm taking a retail job up north, in Cairns. I can start right away. Can you take me to the airport next Wednesday?'

Dara drove Jody across the city to catch her flight. On the way, Jody talked about her new job at a luxury resort hotel. A good wage and they would reimburse her for the flight and accommodation after one month. It was a good deal – she could save way more money than she could at her General Pants job. And no early morning starts either.

'I should have done this a long time ago,' she said as they pulled out onto the freeway, past industrial warehouses and huge shipping containers stacked like box apartments. Big enough for people to live in. She could live out here in one of these – we could live together – Dara thought.

'There is nothing for me here.' Jody's face was drawn, lips pressed in concentration as they passed factories as if trying to take in everything for the last time. She wouldn't let Dara park the car and wait with her in the airline check-in, leaning across to hug her in the driver's seat before she had time to protest. Dara caught her familiar scent – lavender essence, perfume and the faint smell of whiskey – before she climbed out with her suitcase in tow.

'You know if you don't like it you could always walk home!' Dara called from the window as Jody strode toward the sliding airport terminal doors. Jody didn't turn around. Dara couldn't tell if she heard or not.

# Dreamless
## Kim Wilkins

I never dreamed at all, until we moved into the wrecking yard. Old Cooch said that was wrong, that I must have dreamed but I never remembered it. I wasn't sleeping well anymore; dipping in and out with one eye on Peanut. The world of dreams opened up to me, as though I tuned into the channel finally, after eleven years. The birds gave me the first sign.

I was sitting with Old Cooch on the boot of a frontless Kingswood. We were chucking rocks at a line of mismatched bottles on the sun-peeled roof of Cooch's caravan. Peanut was arranging car parts in the dirt, stinky-pants again. I kept telling myself I should change the kid's nappy, but then Cooch would hit another bullseye and taunt me that I hadn't yet hit one.

I was lining up a shot, sure that this time one of the bottles would explode, when a flock of birds flew over head. In an arrow, I guess, but with one arm longer than the other by two birds. I thought, why doesn't one bird go on the other arm, make it even? And a weird feeling washed over me. Memory of something not real. I realised I'd dreamed last night about birds in formations. I actually laughed out loud.

Cooch wanted to know why I laughed and I told him, and that's when he said I'd probably been dreaming my whole life and just didn't know it. But I'd been sleeping in a warm, safe, dreamless bed for most of it, in the house we lived in with Aunty Jemima (who I'm named after even though I'm a boy). When they took Aunty J to the hospital and she didn't come back, when the landlord came and kicked me and Peanut out, that's when we shuffled around town for a day until we came to the wrecking yard. It spread out over two square kilometres, right in the middle of the city. We found an old silver Volvo with no wheels, but it was weather-tight and the seats were leather – luxury! We moved right in. The car smelled of dirt and old bananas, kinda like Peanut, so it felt homey pretty quick. It took less than a day for Cooch to find us; he lived in an abandoned caravan about two-hundred metres away. And even though he was a thief and a liar, it made me feel better to know there was a grown-up close by.

'So what did the birds do in your dream?' Cooch asked, lining up a shot and taking down a VB bottle with pinpoint precision.

I frowned hard, trying to remember. 'They flew over, then they came back. And one dropped dead and landed on the ground right in front of your caravan.'

Cooch had lost interest now, was sniffing Peanut's pants and telling me I needed to change him before he stunk out the whole damn universe. I scooped up Peanut with one arm and he put his chubby hand either side of my face and called me Mimey. I blew a raspberry on his neck and he giggled like it was the funniest thing he'd ever heard, even though I did it, like, eighty times a day. I took him back to the Volvo, wiped his bum and then opened all the doors to air out the car. My tanned fingers with their dirty nails were getting pretty practised at this by now; I could turn almost anything into a nappy: tea towels swiped off washing lines, old jumpers pulled out of Lifeline bins, squares of threadbare blankets left outside the animal shelter. We couldn't afford nappies, and we couldn't afford laundry. I'd had fifty-eight dollars the day Aunty J left, and now I had 42 dollars; and then when that was gone we would be eating out of bins. Peanut's only two. I reckon you have to be minimum four before eating out of bins is okay. He could get sick and he could die, and then I'd have nothing and nobody.

'Jemima! Hey, kid! C'mere!' This was Cooch, shouting at me from where he still sat, splayed knees, on the Kingswood.

'What is it?' I shuffled over. Peanut followed, picking his nose.

Cooch was pointing to a grey shape on the ground in front of his caravan. I picked my way over broken glass, but couldn't make it out until I was nearly on it. A bird. A breeze scuttled over the ground and its feathers moved slightly, almost as though it was breathing. I gave it a poke with my toe. It was impossibly light, and totally dead.

'And?' I asked.

'Those birds came back,' Cooch said, in a cold voice at odds with the blazing hot day. 'This one dropped right out of the sky.'

I looked at him, and my heart thumped a couple of times up near my neck.

'Yeah,' he said, 'just like you dreamed.'

So. Cooch was full of creepy stories and he was a thief and a liar. Probably he found a dead bird and played a joke on me. That would be just like Cooch. When we first met him, he used to go on all the time about the ghosts that prowled the wrecking yard. Trying to get us all worked up. Peanut didn't understand a word, and I just ignored him. Then one night about a week since we'd been there, Cooch came and knocked on our car and he had two hot pizza boxes.

'Come and share, boys,' he said.

Peanut was already asleep but I woke him up because he loves pizza. Cooch told this story about how he'd been walking around town and he found a pizza delivery driver dead at the wheel of his little white car with the fibreglass pizza on top. And Cooch had grabbed the pizzas and brought them back. Who knew if the story was true or not? I had pepperoni juice running down my chin and that's all that mattered. Peanut ate his pizza and started to doze in my lap, and I got talking to Cooch about stuff and he brought up the ghosts again. Only he called them the "wraiths".

'I seen 'em three times now,' he said. 'On every full moon, they come out and they sniff around all the cars and look for people inside. So you've got to be careful that you have your doors closed and your windows up.'

'What do they look like?' I asked.

'Long and black, with scratchy fingers.'

I shrugged it off. He was lying. That's what Cooch did, and he did it well. Making me think I had some kind of psychic dream by planting a dead bird was no surprise and, really, I wasn't scared.


Really late that night – the night after the dead bird – or maybe even it was early the next morning ... anyway, it was dark and I woke up. Dream and reality laid over the top of each other. I'd been dreaming about rain, and here it was raining. But before I could get myself wound up about it, I figured that I'd heard the rain because I was sleeping lightly, and it had made its way into my dream.

I leaned over the back seat to check on Peanut. He was curled up on his side. He'd kicked off his blanket and his arm was hanging off the edge of the seat. The rain drummed on the roof of the car, sluiced off the windows and into the dark nothing outside. I wondered how Cooch was going. He had about six leaks in his caravan. I sat up and peered out, but couldn't see a light on over at his place. Maybe he was just sleeping through it.

I settled back down into my seat, pulling my blanket up even though it was humid and sweaty. I didn't get back to sleep until dawn.


Didn't think about dreams for a while. Perhaps I was getting more comfortable, more used to being eleven years old and responsible for a little kid in nappies. I went into the city a few times and tried to call the hospital where Aunty J was staying, but nobody would tell me anything about her, just that she couldn't see visitors. I guessed whatever sickness she had must be really contagious. I loved my Aunty J, even if she wasn't my real aunty and she smelled like cabbage. Peanut seemed to have forgotten her already. Old Cooch kept saying I need to go see the government people, and tell them I'm living in a car with my two-year-old brother. Aunty J said never trust the government. So I was stuck not knowing what to do and, anyway, we were eating, sleeping, and having kind of a fun time at the wrecking yard with Cooch and all the car parts everywhere. Cooch helped me build a little go-kart, and Peanut pushed himself around in it for hours every day, until his nose was peeling with sunburn. I still had 36 dollars and Peanut started to figure out how to pee against a pole instead of in his pants.

I almost didn't notice the full moon when it came. I've spent my life looking down, not up. But it had been hot for a few days and Peanut and I had taken to playing at night, when it was cooler. He was jumping up and down shouting, 'Mimey, Mimey, my turn!' while I drove the go-kart around (okay, it only actually moved if you were on a slope or if you pushed it with your feet on either side; but it did have a real steering wheel, even if it wasn't attached to anything). I thought, you know it's really light out here tonight and I looked up and saw the cold white moon, just a sliver off being a perfect circle. Cooch had locked himself inside his caravan and wouldn't come out for shouting; but I figured it must be the day he got his government cheque and spent it on booze. We'd see him, blinking in the daylight, in a few mornings, I was sure.

I bundled Peanut up and said it was time for bed. We settled in the car and I opened the driver's side window half way to let some air into the stuffy car. I told Peanut his stories and sang him his songs – such dumb, kiddy songs; he loves them so much – and then he was asleep and I was drifting off too.

That's when I heard a noise. Think of all the words with s's in them that you know, especially the ones that are unpleasant. Slither and slink and hiss. The noise was made up of bits of those words, all joined together in unnatural ways. I sat up, listening, skin prickling. Something scraped across the bottom of the car. I reached across for the window winder, began winding furiously. Something elongated and black began to close over the top of the glass. A finger. Two fingers. I wound. The fingers jerked away; a howl of pain.

I threw myself into the back seat with Peanut, pulled the blanket over the two of us, and breathed. Just breathed. Peanut stirred, whimpered, settled in my arms.

Took me five minutes to figure out it must have been Cooch, playing a trick. *Bastard*. Yeah, Aunty J would hate me to swear but, *bastard*. I'm 11. I'm just a kid. That was a bastard thing to do.

My heart slowed down. A slick of sweat was forming between me and Peanut, but I didn't let him go. We slept, tight against each other, me and my baby brother.


Next day was hot again. Shimmering waves of heat sitting on the dry ground, spearing off old mirrors and windscreens. Peanut found a dead rat by the tyre stacks, and I wondered if it had died of the heat. Cooch didn't come out of his caravan. My stomach started grumbling around eleven. We were out of food, and I knew I'd have to go into the city and get something to eat. I wanted to leave Peanut behind. He was slow and always stopping to look at stuff, then demanding to be carried. I usually left him with Cooch, and even though Cooch was probably drunk and also still a bastard for last night's prank, I went to knock on his caravan door.

Only, as I stood there in front of the door, with my hand raised to knock, I got a horrible feeling. A churning-gut feeling, a raw-throat-burning-heart feeling. I had dreamed this last night. This moment, this body posture, this peeling paint, this *everything*. And the dream, now triggered, came tumbling back fully in my mind. In the dream, Cooch didn't answer and I opened the door. In the dream, I went in and Peanut tried to follow. In the dream, the floor of the caravan was awash with blood. In the dream, the wrecking yard wraiths had been in, and they'd finished off Old Cooch.

I didn't want to knock.

'Mimey?' Peanut said.

I turned. 'Go back to the car, okay? I'll come get you.'

He kicked a rock and sat down in the dirt, but didn't go back to the car. I told myself I was being a baby. I told myself dreams don't come true. I knocked hard. The door opened a crack, under the force of my knock. My breath got stuck in my throat.

'Cooch?' I called in a baby voice that made me ache with embarrassment for myself. 'Hey, Old Cooch,' I tried again, manlier. 'You there?'

He was probably drunk, that was all. I pushed the door all the way in.

Blood. Everywhere.

I pushed the scream all the way back down; I pushed it so hard that it got stuck in my stomach. I wanted to run and never stop running, but Cooch was the only grown-up I had. I took a step inside, another, couldn't see his body. Peanut was suddenly there, at the door, calling to me.

'No, Peanut!' I cried, turning to shoo him away from the caravan. My foot slid in the blood, I came crashing down on my elbows, face to face with Cooch's dead eyes.

Peanut began to cry. I scrabbled to my feet. Cooch was under the table, head hanging by a flap. Something had torn out his throat. I launched myself towards Peanut, I didn't want him to see any of this. I tackled him to the ground outside the van – the sun shone hard, not scared of a thing. Peanut cried louder. I picked him up and took him back to our car. Popped the boot and got out clean, blood-free clothes for us.

'Peanut,' I said, as I pushed his little hands and elbows through the armholes of a fresh t-shirt, 'we've got to go to the city. We've got to see the government people.'

'Gubberment,' he echoed solemnly.

'Yeah, kid,' I said. 'It's not right for two little boys to be living here.'

We left the car behind and headed for the city.

Oh, yeah. The city. The big shiny pointing-to-the-sky city, all glittering with money and heartlessness. Everybody gliding from place to place in their fine clothes. Well, all except Peanut and me in bare feet and clothes last-year-too-small; both of us kind of crab-crawling because I had to chase Peanut as he followed his baby instincts into anything he'd never seen before, which was practically everything. I eventually had to pick him up and carry him, all achy-arms, through the hushed sliding doors of the government building.

The aircon hit my skin like ice, and I immediately felt less of a savage. The whole place was white. White floor, white walls, white furniture. Like nobody ever felt anything here. Peanut found some empty forms to scribble on, and I filled one out too, to take up to the counter.

Name: *Jemima and Peanut*

Address: *the silver Volvo next to tyre stack, city wrecking yard*

Next of kin:

I scratched my head. A lady with white hair pulled back so tight it made her eyes tilt up at the corners came over.

'Are you all right?'

I turned. 'Um ... me and my brother have nobody to look after us, and I'm pretty sure something bad's going to happen.'

Her eyebrows lifted half a millimetre. 'Where are your parents?'

I shrugged.

'Your guardian then?'

'Aunty J's been looking after us. I don't know my parents. I only remember her.'

The woman indicated Peanut. 'Then where did your brother come from?'

'He just turned up one day.'

I heard the sliding doors open and close, quiet voices, people with manners and houses talking to each other.

'And where is your Aunty J now?' the woman said.

'She's in hospital for a while.'

She nodded. She could work with this. She reached for a phone. 'I see, and which hospital?'

'Galloway.'

This time, she physically recoiled. 'Galloway isn't a hospital.'

Right then Peanut came barrelling into me, nearly knocking me over. He held up a page of scribbles proudly.

'Hey, that's great,' I said, just like Aunty J would say to me when I drew a picture.

The woman had beckoned over another worker, a tall man who watched over her shoulder.

'How old is your brother?' she asked, punching keys on her computer.

'He turned two in November.'

'I'll see if I can get him into an infant care facility right away. As for you, you might have to spend a week with a foster family, until we can transport you out to a farm home.'

I shook my head. 'Peanut and me, we're brothers. We've got to stay together.'

Her pupils contracted. 'Forgive me, but you don't know your parents or his. You don't even look alike. I doubt that you are brothers.'

'Aunty J always said we were.'

She sighed, turned to the man next to her and said, under her breath, 'Aunty J is in a prison for the criminally insane.'

I clutched Peanut, helpless. This wasn't part of the deal, us getting split up. The woman looked intently at her computer screen and said. 'We can't get a case worker here to talk to you until tomorrow. As for tonight ...'

I thrust the form across at her, trying not to think about Old Cooch dead and roasting in his caravan. 'I'll take care of Peanut. Our address is on here. We can manage one more night. Just make sure they come tomorrow, okay?'

On the walk home, I held Peanut close against me as long as I could, but he got so heavy and I was horribly aware that I just had little-kid arms, little-kid brains. I didn't even know what 'criminally insane' meant, at least not what the words meant together like that. Tonight we would sleep in the car, and I would make sure all the locks were locked and all the windows were wound up tight – don't think about Cooch, doing the same thing on his caravan – and it didn't matter if it got to thirty degrees I would sleep with Peanut in my arms. And I wouldn't let anybody, no wrecking-yard wraith no Gubberment case-worker, take him away from me.

*Dreaming feels like being half-connected, feels like being lost in patterns pretending to be real things. In this dream, I wake up in the back of the old Volvo, and I look down and Peanut isn't in my arms. There's an old blanket instead, rolled up and empty. The driver's door is open and I think, it's all my fault because I couldn't drive. There is a trail of blood, thin and dark, over the door and awful spots of it on the dusty ground outside, and the sniffing, snuffling sound of something — not a dog, not a man, not anything natural to this world - just ...*

There!

I sat up with every nerve in my body alight. I looked down. Peanut, still in my arms. His eyes were closed but his eyeballs were moving around underneath; he was dreaming too. I listened into the dark, but heard nothing.

Nothing.

Nothing but – oh, shit – the dream.

That was two hours ago. I'm pretty sure that it's about midnight now. All I have to do is stay awake until dawn because if I don't fall asleep, it can't happen, right? I can't wake up to find Peanut gone if I don't sleep in the first place.

But I'm so tired. My eyelids are lined with lead. I'm weak. I'm just a kid, though I hate to admit it. I want to be big: big enough to survive the loss of Aunty Jemima, and big enough to live in a car, and big enough to stay awake all night, and big enough to protect Peanut. But I am a child.

And dawn is so, so far away.

# Dreamless [Super-Villanelle Dub Mix]
## Sean Williams

big enough to stay awake
I've taken to playing at night
dawn is so, so far away.

brought up the ghosts again
peer out, but can't see a light
big enough to stay awake

go back to the car, okay?
every nerve in my body alight
dawn is so, so far away.

I push the scream all the way
pretty sure it's about midnight
big enough to stay awake

at odds with the blazing hot day
windows are wound up tight
dawn is so, so far away.

all I have to do is stay awake
we can manage one more night.
big enough to stay awake
dawn is so, so far away.

# Dreamless [Super-Villanelle Dub Alternate Mix]
## Sean Williams

gliding from place to place
I realised I'd dreamed last night
a baby voice that made me ache

he just turned up one day
he was impossibly light
gliding from place to place

little-kid arms, little-kid brains
dropped right out of the sky
a baby voice that made me ache

joined together in unnatural ways
big enough to stay awake all night
gliding from place to place

shuffled around town for a day
don't fall asleep, it can't happen, right?
a baby voice that made me ache

eating out of bins is okay
I have taken to playing at night.
gliding from place to place
a baby voice that made me ache

# How to Domesticate a Pirate
## Danielle Wood

Step onto a ship wearing a small black dress that is not enough to protect you from a wind that blows colder over water than it does over land. It forces you to seek warmth in the radiance of a man whose bare feet have the same rough-hardness as deck timber and who smells of brine and varnish. In his sunbrowned face his smile is a white cutlass. His eyes, predictably, are blue. Issue an invitation, but do not wait for it to be accepted. Look back over your shoulder as you walk the plank. Say *I'll be expecting you.*

Get used to being caressed by hands that make you feel as rare and precious as other things they've touched, like the horny shell of Jonathan the tortoise, who walked St Helena with Napoleon, and the purple hearts of ebony trees, both king and queen. Learn to fuck in a hammock, you on top, taut fabric curling like another skin around your knees and calves and feet. Fall in love with the feeling of poems reeling out of you like tunes out of his battered fiddle, some of them as bright and brief as phosphorescence, others as thick and durable as rope. You hope that in years hence you will be able to suck on these and still taste salt water.

When the time is right, begin to lure him ashore. Suggest a tent rather than a house (at this stage) and spend a year's worth of dawns in its pitched glow-worm green. The poems from this time are, like your sheets, stained with pindan. You will never be able to wash it out, but nor would you want to.

Now accept a proposal of marriage that is offered to you on the palm of a hand, along with a freshly-shucked oyster. But then push your canoe away from the rocks, over the aqua shallows to the navy depths where you couldn't hear even if someone were shouting at you to come back to shore. Ostensibly, you don't like weddings. But out here, you wrestle with the Barbie doll sector of your soul. The part that tries to seduce you by whispering crimplene thoughts and scattering fake rose petals at your feet. You try to drown her, but her synthetic hair doesn't hold water and her plastic hollow limbs just keep bobbing to the surface.

Acquire a house, and jobs that mean you can pay for it and all the things it must contain. Oh brave new world! Who would have imagined the glory of choosing exactly the right bath tap! Each new purchase generates an invisible computer code, and the multiplying sequences of numbers encircle you, locking you tight to the world of debt.

Next, bear a child with blue eyes. Suspect that he, too, will grow to think of your poems as the elaborate talking of shit; will learn to smile with baffled indulgence at your finely wrought lines. Know that you are doomed to love him – unconditionally, painfully, gratefully – anyway.

Wonder whether you will ever again write poetry, now that your mind is full of so much else. Else, else, else. There is nothing but else in your head these days, and else is all the language that is left between you and the man who comes home to you each night now in a suit. will the nappies last until Saturday?

Optus or Telstra?

what if interest rates rise?

is the car service due?

who wormed the dog?

accumulation or defined benefit?

when *is* enough enough?

The else is like packing foam, insubstantial and expansive. Your head is crammed with little dimples of it that are the same shape and colour as prawn crackers, but quite a bit smaller. Or else the else is like popcorn, clouding and crowding with sudden inflations. Soon cumulus pieces begin to tumble out of the holes of your ears.

Stand in a supermarket queue and pass judgement. Here, you catch yourself despising a woman in beige three-quarter pants because she has filled her trolley with her own sub-urbanity. And because, when she talks to her toddler, she refers to herself in the third person. But when you – in your internal voice – mock her, you sound just like yourself.

You suspect you might be depressed but find yourself too pathetic to admit it. Nightly on the news American grenades explode brownskinned families while Australian tourists fuck little seven-year-old Thai boys up the arse while the planet coughs up its diminishing oil reserves so that humanity can fry itself and here in your middle class house in your first world country with your husband and your child and your fabric softener, you're crying about *what* exactly?

When your husband comes out of the bedroom in the morning and asks you a question, and you find yourself paralysed by its malice-less venom, know that you deserve it. That you've asked for it. That you've had it coming. That you carried the seeds of it on the hem of your small black dress, that you glimpsed the grit of it in the mucousy flesh of that oyster, that you allowed it to be slipped onto your finger, that you grew it in your womb, applied to the bank for it, wrote it on the shopping list for Saturday. When he asks again, because he thinks you haven't heard, don't cry for your pirate and his roughbare feet and cutlass smile. Don't over-react. He only wants to know if you've ironed his shirt yet.

# How to Domesticate a Pirate [Live Fed Square Remix]
## Mark Lawrence

Get used to being caressed by hands that make you feel as rough and hard as deck timber.

Stand in a supermarket queue and pass judgement. You catch yourself despising a woman in beige three-quarter pants because she has filled her trolley with

interest rates
the car service
defined benefit
and your fabric softener.

And because, when she talks to her toddler, she refers to herself in the third person.

Who wormed the dog?

Else, else, else. There is nothing but else in your head these days, and else is all the language that is left between you and the man who now comes home to you each night in a suit.

When your husband comes out of the bedroom in the morning and asks you a question, grenades explode.

He only wants to know if you've ironed his shirt yet.
Will you push your canoe away from the rocks, over the aqua shallows, to the navy depths where you couldn't hear even if someone were shouting at you to come back to shore?

No, the nappies can't last until Saturday.

# How to Domesticate a Pirate [What if if only Remix]

**Amelia Schmidt**

Else, else, else.
will the nappies last until Saturday?
Optus or Telstra?
what if interest rates rise?
is the car service due?
who wormed the dog?
accumulation or defined benefit?
when is enough enough?

She wonders whether she will ever again write poetry, now that her mind is full of so much else. There is nothing but else in her head these days, and else is all the language that is left between her and the man who comes home to her each night now in a suit.

Oh brave new world!
Who would have imagined
the glory of choosing
exactly the right bath tap!
Nightly on the news
American grenades

When her husband comes out of the bedroom in the morning and asks her a question, and she finds herself paralysed by its malice-less venom, she knows that she deserves it. That she's asked for it. That she's had it coming. That she carried the seeds of it on the hem of her small black dress, that she glimpsed the grit of it in the mucousy flesh of that oyster, that she allowed it to be slipped onto her finger, that she grew it in her womb, applied to the bank for it, wrote it on the shopping list for Saturday. She doesn't over-react. He only wants to know if she's ironed his shirt yet.

explode brownskinned families
while Australian tourists
fuck little seven-year-old Thai boys

> up the arse while the planet coughs up
> its diminishing oil reserves

The else is like packing foam, insubstantial and expansive. Her head is crammed with little dimples of it that are the same shape and colour as prawn crackers, but quite a bit smaller. Or else the else is like popcorn, clouding and crowding with sudden inflations. Soon cumulus pieces begin to tumble out of the holes of your ears. The poems from this time are, like her sheets, stained with clouds. She will never be able to wash it out, but nor would she want to.

> so that humanity can
> fry itself and here
> in your middle class house
> in your first world country

She suspects she might be depressed but finds herself too pathetic to admit it, so instead she stands in a supermarket queue and passes judgement. Here, she catches herself despising a woman in beige three-quarter pants because she has filled her trolley with her own sub-urbanity. And because, when this woman talks to her toddler, she refers to herself in the third person. But when she – in her internal voice – mocks another, she sounds just like ... you.

> with your husband
> and your child
> and your fabric softener,
> you're crying about what exactly?

Of course, though, she isn't the person that she was expecting – she says, *I never expected you*. Stares at herself in the mirror, puts on a dress she's not even looked at for twenty years. Ignores the crows' feet that she said one day she'd do something about, remember the colour of the sea and how much it looked like her eyes that day. Thinks of the sound of the sand under the bottoms of your crunch-crunching shoes.

She experiences the strangeness of your childhood and your future blending together in a long stretch of white sand along an azure coastline, contrasting like a postcard only your imagination can send.

Puts down her Tupperware and stops the violent beating blades of the machinery in the kitchen for one quiet moment and realises that the beach is only down the road. That the sun shining through the fly-screens shines down on to the shells and the waves and that it reflects in splashes of bright, bright, blinding white as the sound of the seas hungry for shorelines wells up and down.

She leaves a note, but does not wait for it to be accepted. Looks back over her shoulder at the sad eyes of a thirteen-year-old boy whose mother can't keep herself ashore. Looks back over her shoulder at the suburban boulevard, all grey and grey and green and white, as it disappears into a fractal pattern of a city. Looks back over her shoulder as she walks the plank.

My eyes, predictably, are blue. In my sunbrowned face this smile is a white cutlass. It forces her to seek warmth in the radiance of this man whose bare feet have the same rough-hardness as deck timber and who smells of brine and varnish.

So she steps onto *my* ship wearing a small black dress that is not enough to protect her from a wind that blows colder over water than it does over land. So I offer her a hat and a shirt, and wonder whether one day she, like us, will feel the dull longing for the land and sand between her toes. I ask her which way a lady wishes to sail, and she stares off towards the horizon. When I ask again, because I think she hasn't heard, she won't cry for a pirate and his roughbare feet. She'll have him, and nothing else.

Else, else, else.
will the rations last until Saturday?
North or South?
what if the tides rise?
are the sails due for mending?
where's that mangy mongrel?
scenic or direct route?
a mariner knows no limits.
Oh brave new world!
Who would have imagined
the glory of choosing
exactly the right course to follow!
Nightly we tell stories

Of how our gunfire
exploded brownskinned families
while coast-born landlubbers
took wenches to their dives,
bought them jewels and
rare treasures from ruined worlds
so that brave men of the ocean can
burn their noses bright
on the salt-stained deck
in the new, undiscovered worlds
with their lasses and broads
and their foundlings
and some rough, dirty rags
to wipe their homesick tears.

# Renovator's Heaven

## Cate Kennedy

Colin's up, he's been up for hours. Lay in bed at dawn thinking about preparing the woodwork, now he's got the colour sample cards and he's thinking it over. He's considering. Bayleaf? Firtree? Eucalypt Forest?

The three greens swim together. When he blinks he sees rectangles of pink ghosting before his eyelids. He blinks rapidly, tucks the samples away. He'll think about it later. Plenty of time to get it exactly right.

It's still a pleasure to stand out on the verandah, running his hand occasionally over the handcut eaves. Christ! How much timber had he discarded before he got that perfect? And the fitting! The chiselling and clamping! The slow wiping away of the bead of glue, the ache in his neck as he sanded with the finest grade paper. Some other craftsman in the future, Colin thinks absently, is going to pull a stepladder under these eaves and do a double take when they realise how they're made. He's invited friends round, pointed stuff out to them. *It's a labour of love*, he's told them, following their eyes around the ornate cornices and hand-stripped dado. *Sure it takes time and effort, but, well ...* and here he's made himself trail off with a wry, resigned smile, a poet's helpless gesture of perfection.

*Look at this*, he'd said, pulling open kitchen-cupboard doors lined in baltic tongue-and-groove. *Had to strip all that down.* He couldn't help himself. *You can't use a machine for detail like that – you've got to do it all by hand.* Taking the drawer out entirely and showing them the dovetailing he'd repaired.

It had been the For-Sale sign that had hooked him, the Sunday he'd come round for the auction, a year ago.

'Renovator's Heaven!' it had said. 'Needs the Touch of a Skilled Craftsman to Restore to its Former Glory.'

And Colin was the man. Not everyone had it in them, but he did. When he raised his hand to bid, he did so gravely, like a man earnest with the responsibility bestowed upon him. Now he goes inside and snaps on the kettle for his fifth coffee of the day. He's tending towards Eucalypt Forest now, but there's plenty of time to decide. There's a clearing sale of building materials on, he's seen in the paper, on the other side of the city, but they'd listed Edwardian windows, and Colin's pretty confident he'd find some usable glass panels in them if he went. He's got a few stacked in the garage; more than he can use at present, truth be known, but they just didn't make glass like that any more and it never hurts to have proper materials in reserve for new projects. That makes sense to a craftsman but try telling that to his bitch of an ex-wife. Colin's got brackets running up the walls in the garage, stacked with tongue-and-groove Baltic pine boards, the wides and the narrows, and sometimes he just goes in there and does an inventory of how much he has and how much floor he could replace if needed. It's a good feeling, being prepared for anything. So there's the decision on the paint, and there's the clearing sale option, and perhaps he could swing past the Restorer's Warehouse on his way home. He's confident that if he just strolls around the garden, he'll come across something that needs doing, something that will pull the day into an ordered and useful shape. He'd lain in bed last night and listened to the wind gust across the roof, and felt the pleasurable anticipation of checking the roofing iron the next day. Just that worrisome spot he's had his eye on, where he's replaced a piece on the diagonal.

*Don't overdo it*, his doctor had advised early on, frowning and examining the rash Colin had got up his arms after heat-stripping off layers of lead-based paint in the bathroom. *You're no spring chicken.* He'd loosened the blood-pressure cuff and rubbed his chin at the result. *Just take it slowly, you've got all your retirement for renovating, right?* Idiot. Like he was some kind of amateur do-it-yourselfer.

Colin sniffs and picks up the claw-hammer and goes up the ladder onto the roof. It's windy up there; best not to stand upright. Best to crawl carefully pushing your boots against the washers of the roofing screws. All perfectly aligned. He inserts the tip of the claw hammer under the suspect flap.

Rust. He's not imagining it. Three red marks of rust.

It's not that he's scared of heights. It's just sensible to back down crabwise to the last sheet of iron and feel the guttering with your boot, make sure it's solid as a rock before you put any weight on it. No, it's not heights; the wind chill would make anyone's heart work overtime up here. That's good, useful adrenaline. Eighteen rungs and then the ground. Then into the laundry for the new silicone-gun, then back to seal these spots, and he won't have to climb the ladder again till Autumn. The thought of the rust irritating him like prickly heat, hard to keep your mind on anything else once you knew it was there, eating away your roof.

Five steps down, he has one of his giddy turns. A stab of pain rises and recedes, the roofline skews, and Colin's vision drenches red for a few seconds. The world tears grey and papery around the edges. Then it clears: a familiar rising horizon of galvanised iron, ladder set firm against the eave, the coppery aftertaste in his mouth.

When he opens his eyes, the light is dazzling. He climbs down, shaking, his legs turned cottony and weak, like he suddenly weighs nothing.


As he collects his mail he happened to glance down the road. Strange. He can't remember that old Edwardian place six doors up being renovated, but there's the blue garbage skip out the front, piled full.

He strolls down to investigate. The house is finished but deserted, glittering with fresh paint. Colin's heart jumps and squirms. Inside the skip there's a pair of French doors. Perfect condition, not even the glass broken. Thrown out! That hardly seems possible, but here they are, tipped sideways into the mouth of the bin, some snapped framing timbers stacked on top.

Colin swallows, fingers his tape measure. He's already modifying what he feels he's entitled to expect here, already readying himself for disappointment with a small knowing smile, because stuff like this, that you just happened across, never turns out to be really exactly what you wanted. Like as not, in Colin's experience, the work you had to put in getting them right ends up costing you as much as getting them custom-made anyway, like these doors for example, there was no way they would be 1.85 metres, which was the odd size he's planning on getting custom-built for his sunroom. But even as he's talking himself out of it, he's pulling out the tape, hands trembling a bit, and measuring them.

1.85 metres.

Colin glances around. He could get these home right now and have them in by the end of the day. Even the hinges are perfect. He tries to lift one, and fails with a grunt. Weigh a ton, of course – quality old wood. His mind's starting to race, wondering who could he call on to give him a hand. He knows almost nobody in the street, hadn't had the time to socialise. Too busy with the house and getting his affairs in order and one thing and another. The place seems deserted, anyway. Like the builders have finished the job and just left, and cut their losses and left these valuable doors ...

Colin's squinting down the street when he notices the other blue skip at the corner. He has to blink a few times to focus on what's filling it, because the light this morning seems headache-bright somehow, all glancing dazzle and flash like the surface of water, but he clears his vision as he hurries down there, seeing timber stacked and upended inside. He's smiling again, preparing himself, as he jogs down. Probably rotten floorboards.

But he gets there and puts his hand on it, and he can't believe it but it's kiln-dried cypress, looking brand-new. No nailholes, no nothing.

Colin feels beads of sweat collecting, slippery, under his hat. Worth a fortune, worth several dollars a metre, he knows that for a fact, and his for the taking. Enough for the doorframes and the yawning hole in the laundry wall where he'd impulsively taken out the old copper. Enough to take home right now and get started. It's Renovator's Heaven out here today, Holy God.

He wipes his mouth, trying to think if there's anybody with a truck he could borrow. Or just a flat-bed ute, and someone to help him out. *Wonder if I could take up half an hour of your time*, Colin would say, extending his hand. *Just couldn't help noticing up the road ...*

Couldn't help noticing another skip.

Colin's mouth is rank from all that coffee. It tastes as if he's had nails clamped between his lips, or coins. His arms and legs, though, feel like he's been hanging on to something huge and jolting and percussive, like a jackhammer. He hurries to this one. It's a house he doesn't think he's noticed before, double-fronted Victorian, weedy front garden. The verandah's been left, sagging, in the process of being pulled off.

Thrown carelessly into the skip, unbelievably, is more wrought-iron than he's ever seen. His hands scrabble at it. He needs help. By Christ, he needs to race back home for his trailer and try to haul this stuff home before the owners wake up to themselves. He can pull it out himself, one piece at a time, he's sure of it. And maybe if he gets some ropes he can pull the doors out too, slide them to the ground somehow, pay someone to come and ...

Colin sucks on the metallic sharpness in his mouth, trying to swallow dryness, blinking again to clear his blurred vision in the bright glare, because he can't help but shade his eyes and look further down the road. He can't believe the road's so long, now he comes to think about it; it's always seemed like a smallish suburban street to him, but here it is, stretching away, all the way to the intersection, and when he squints he can see them lined up, bang, bang, bang, in cubes of unmistakable aqua blue. Skip after skip.

Colin stumbles along at a half-jog, his breath rasping. How can he begin to catalogue what's in those skips, how can he even start to plan?

He sees windows, stacked against another skip, genuine rolled-glass six-pane windows, the kind with brass snibs you can't buy anymore. Boxes of deco tiles. A pedestal sink with original old taps, even the porcelain heads; he's only ever seen pictures of those. And they're in skips, these treasures. Without him, they're all headed for the tip. To be dropped by machines onto mountains of garbage, splintering and warping and shattering. It's criminal. Unthinkable. Colin runs back towards his place, his nerves jangling, and inside his chest anxiety and desire twist and flex together into one unbearable clenching torment. He's winded with it, aching. Maybe that's it, maybe he's feverish, horrified by the thought of losing, the prospect of missing any of it. And here's his own house, every inch of it his, but suddenly so bitterly unfinished, so needful of everything he's seen waiting for him. Jerked to a halt there, he hears something which soaks him in a fresh flush of sweat, although he's staring with such blank horror at what lies crumpled on the grass at the base of his ladder that his mind can't attend to it at first. One horror at a time, says his brain, just take in one thing. That noise. That could only be the worst possible thing, the skip-company's truck, coming to collect. He hears it pull up at the first distant skip with a kind of delirious panic, hears the hydraulic hoist grab it and the faint, delicate sound of glass tinkling, timber frames bursting under impact. Not delirious, his brain registers, sorting. And not the worst possible thing, either. That would be what he can't drag his eyes from. The thing that lies sprawling at the foot of the ladder, still resting against the eave. The thing in his shirt. Not delirious, because it's still clutching the claw-hammer, and Colin for the life of him can't remember what he'd done with it when he'd got down. He swallows back the whimper in his throat, gazes wildly round.

It occurs to him again, the horrible bright silent strangeness of it.

There's not another soul in sight.

# Renovator's Heaven [Renovator's Hell Remix]
## Amra Pajalic

'Look at these ornate cornices,' Kirsty, his wife's best friend and their real estate agent, pointed out the verandah. They were getting a sneak peak inspection before the property went on the market.

'Nice,' Lisa, his wife said, looking down the street. Her sole interest was location, location, location, and this was one of the best streets in the suburb.

'Why is the property on the market?' he asked Kirsty as she unlocked the front door.

'The owner retired.'

He was in the kitchen when he felt Lisa standing beside him. 'This is handmade,' he said, running his hands over the kitchen cupboard doors lined in Baltic tongue and groove. He looked up, but he was alone.

The garage had brackets running up the walls, stacked with pine boards, and Edwardian windows in the corner.

'All this will be disposed of before the house goes on the market,' Kirsty said.

'You can use these to finish renovations,' Lisa whispered.

He smiled, internally wincing. He hated renovating. Whenever he started out a home project it never came off the way he imagined it.

Kirsty left them in the backyard to deliberate. 'It's perfect,' Lisa said, her smile brimming with excitement as she squeezed his arm.

'I'm not sure if it's us,' he remembered the creeping sensation while he'd inspected the house. 'Don't you like the modern look more?'

'Yes, but we can rip out all the traditional fittings.'

He hesitated, looking at the house behind them. On the surface the house was perfect for them. It met all the check-boxes on their wish-list, but there was something not quite right.

'Don't you like it?' Lisa took hold of his hand.

Seeing the disappointment on her face he couldn't take away her joy. Anyway what could he say?

'You're right,' he put his arm around her shoulders and led her back inside. 'It's perfect.'

It began on the day they moved in. At first it was so small he barely noticed it. He put his Coke on the windowsill in the living room. When he went to take a drink, he found the bottle in the kitchen. He assumed Lisa had taken a sip and moved it.

But as days passed, his unease deepened. Things would move when he was alone in the house. He felt a malevolent presence following him from room to room, watching over as he undertook any repair job. His tools would short-circuit every time he used them. When he asked Lisa if she felt anything strange, she smiled, like he was a child telling a tall tale.

He was setting up the ladder to fix the television antenna, disturbed by high winds, when a neighbour walked past. After they exchanged hellos the neighbour lingered.

'Be careful on the ladder,' the neighbour said. 'That's how the previous owner found his end.'

After the neighbour left he took the ladder back to the shed. When Lisa turned on the TV and the reception was still off, he lied and said he'd attempted to fix it. The next day he went through the local paper looking for an antenna repair man.

He saw an advertisement for a medium claiming to dispose of problem spirits. He cut it out and placed it in his wallet.

That night the dreams started. There was a shadowy presence standing over his bed. He'd try to move, but an invisible force held him down. He woke gasping for breath, his muscles atrophied and taking minutes to respond to his commands.

He got in touch with the medium. Pretending to leave for work, he drove around the corner, called in sick and returned home after Lisa left.

When the medium entered the house her eyes fluttered. 'I feel the chill of a recent death and the heat of an unsettled spirit.'

She lit candles and formed a circle, claiming a purification ceremony would force the spirit to leave. 'The ceremony will only work if you believe,' she sat cross-legged on the floor.

He joined her, goosepimples rising on his skin as the candles fluttered. He felt the familiar malevolent presence beside him. A force gripped him, squeezing his body so he couldn't breathe. He tried to scream, but no sound came out. A veil descended between him and the house as if he was looking through the world under water.

'Much better,' his voice said, but he didn't think the words. He tried to ask the medium what had happened, but his mouth didn't respond.

After the medium left he walked through the house examining the shoddy workmanship from his amateur attempts at renovation. He collected the power tools and tossed them in the skip out the back.

'You can't use a machine for detail like that – you've got to do it all by hand.'

# Renovator's Heaven [Free Verse Sonnet Remix]
## Phillip Ellis

Colin Feels Beads to Order

----------------------

Flush of sweat, although he's staring with such
blank horror. He, Colin's mouth is rank from
all that coffee. Here they are, tipped sideways
into perfect. He tries the left, sagging,
in the process of vision as he hurries
down there, seeing timber unthinkable.
Colin hammers, under the suspect flap,
cards, and he's in them thinking it over.
He's considering the suspect flap. Rust,
put in getting them right ends Sunday that
he'd come. That would be what he can't work; you
had, like as not, in Colin's experience,
the work a metre: he knows that for a
fact, and his thing that lies sprawling on floorboards.

# 'Soliloquy for one dead'
## James Phelan

That they were both named Nigel is a distant memory, flotsam fading away. For now, it's the smells of barbecues and cut grass that blow their way, the adventure that lies ahead. These two friends, Jim and Joe, leave their homes and chores behind to ride through evening streets. The sun, still strong, heats their backs as they joke and laugh and weave. Kids are ganging, playing cricket and hopscotch down lanes and dodging cars. Teenagers fix Fords and Holdens kerb-side, INXS's new anthem blazing.

Down Church Street the pair meet up with the Yarra, the wind up their tail as a group launches stones at them. They whoop and fang along the riverbank, taking their worn track in the couch grass as if they were late for the time of their lives. Matching haircuts flow blond, skin tanned from the long summer, smiles flash white.

Shorts and t-shirts on the ground, Joe unties a book from his bike and shows his friend.

Treasure Island, Joe says. You read it?

Not like that, just one with pictures. Dad read it to me, couple of years ago, Jim says.

Take it in turns to read the chapters? Joe flicks through the old hard cover as he speaks, appraising the time ahead.

Sure. Jim pats his mate on the arm and walks nearer the edge. He's prone, ready to pounce. But first, we fly!

Joe hides the book amongst their clothes and pushes the bikes into a tangle of banksia.

Ready, Joe?

Joe stands to, crouches like a sprinter.

Ready, Jim.

They run full pelt and leap into the sky, leaving the Earth for a while.

Splash! They drop like cannonballs, entering the water from the heavens.

Jim paddles to the black wattle root he always uses to haul himself out, not at home in the liquid like his mate. He looks up the sheer face of Notts Point, beaming at his – their – courage. Another few jumps and they'll have to find a higher place to fly from. He straightens his jocks and turns around. Scoops up clay to throw at Joe.

Jim scans, eyes darting, up and down, left to right. Eyes widen. Smiles. Joe swims underwater, bobbing up where Jim least expects it. Almost on the other side once, where the sad peppercorn dips into the water.

Several heartbeats pass. Jim's hand is still raised, ready to piff the clay.

He's wishing he had his shanghai, but glad he didn't bring it down – he'd lost his change on their first jump, a couple of weeks ago, having stuffed it down his jocks. The week's paper round money, gone. The river was like that, taking things, never to return from that muck that went forever down.

His arm shakes, tired, raised above his head, slung back and ready to fire.

The smile remains. Movement – he launches. Fish. Should bring their rods next time; no one fishes here, the fish'd be real dumb.

He stands, unarmed, and feels suddenly alone.

Joe? Joe!

He squints to see through the peppercorn's curtain, squats to peep under.

Come on, dickhead! he says, kicking his foot through the water. The ripples eddy out, expanding fast, breaking at a snag in its curve.

Joe?

Jim slips into the warm brown water that envelops his body, a womb.

There's no riverbed here, at least not one a ten-year-old can reach, and he wades to the snag that continues to break the ripples of his entry. His breath holds, he looks, taking it in. Pale. Soft. Skin. A finger, just breaching the surface. Jim sputters. In five years all he'd known was laughs with Joe. A heat rushes up his neck and flares in his jocks.

Jim pulls at his mate's hand. Tugs. Thrashes about with the effort.

C'mon! He moves closer, can feel his submerged friend against his body, still. His feet find ground and he stands on something hard, smooth, metallic. Foreign. He tugs at an arm, puts his head under and gets some leverage.

He sees Joe in a car – almost sitting in the back seat. Bent through the shattered window. It's dark down there but the image of the familiar illuminates.

Forever.

Jim goes to high school, the year glides into winter, and then time stands still. Days drag and weeks sigh to a close, leaving emptiness all round the twelve-year-old. The walks home are long despite the distance, and he's sodden by the time he comes through the door. His mother can't believe he could lose three umbrellas in as many weeks, not realising the barbarism of teenage boys. Bruises go unnoticed.

Home becomes quiet, his parents no longer fighting into the night. His father not home before dark, drinking beer in the garage if he is. Jim sits at his homework with headphones blaring Nirvana, defeating the silence. Little gets done.

Before the winter breaks, his mother packs the Volvo and takes him and the cat down the coast.

We're staying with Nan for a while, she tells him. Thank God they didn't have more kids, Jim thinks, feeling able to brave whatever happened next. He's grown used to being alone, and is sure his mum will too. He feels stronger, like he has something to give. Dry again, lighter.

I was raped.

His mother decides to break the silence after the Tracy Chapman tape ends by articulating what she'd always wanted to say. Jim feels the heat rise up his neck again, his throat closing, the weight of it all.

Why are you telling me that?

I thought you should know. A few years after you were born. While your father and I were apart for a while. I had a really hard time when you were young.

Jim stares at a chip in the windscreen the rest of the car trip, all silent tears and clenched fists.


Three years pass to become an endless summer.

Jim finds friends, discovers laughs and smiles again, gets some colour back. He still thinks of Joe, how they used to share and talk about books, reading their favourite bits aloud. His new friends play football and surf, shoot things and ride motorbikes. He misses not knowing someone who reads, but he can look back differently now. He's finding himself.

At night, Jim lays on the concrete water tank, watching the Milky Way shift in the pitch blackness that surrounds their home. On a far-off horizon is the haze of Melbourne, an eerie glow as if the place is on fire or a nuclear bomb has gone off. He's glad he's out of there, sure it's safer from the end of the world where he is.

Tony becomes his new best friend – an Italian kid who lives on a farm. Jim respects the confines of Tony's limitations, and anything outside that takes him by surprise. At home, Jim still listens to Nirvana through headphones, reads books on the bus as it snakes the dirt roads, adapts his life for this new companionship. Sport takes hold, Aussie Rules and cycling, shooting and camping. His mate talks of tractors and farm yields, peas and cows. Jim declines swimming in dams, even when it's thirty-plus. Tony chides him for it. Jim watches the clouds until he hears his mate is out.

You need to eat more! the Italian mother tells Jim.

I eat, Jim says. We're pretty poor though, he thinks rather than adds.

Not that there isn't food on the table ... just not the snacks that his mate has a constant supply of. That morning bucket of cow's milk from the dairy next door. The grocery budget.

You're so skinny, Mrs Italy is relentless. Jim studies his empty plate and wonders what else he could have done, and his friend excuses them from the table so they can shoot foxes at dusk.

Jim laughs when his mother recites Mrs Italy's two phrases uttered her way so far: Show me your kitchen ... oh. So why'd you leave his father?

His mum voices these and laughs, but Jim feels the pain of it for them both.

Jim is asked by no fewer than eight girls to the debutante ball. It's the girl's right to ask the boy, and he figures he must have some kind of city kid novelty factor working his way. He grows tired of saying no, loses track of who's asked him, and when Tony says he's got a date organised, Jim relents.

She's tall like him, blonde and thoughtful. Not in the surfer crowd, or the rich list, the geeks or the alternative lot. They're so similar it's destined to turn into something, and without knowing it Jim is going out with her and at risk of losing another good friend.

Jim kisses her after school one day. It's his first, all clumsy and feverish. She says it's her first too, and that seems important to him. He thinks she flinches on contact.

They sit together in class and hold hands after school. Jim trades off the stigma of being the only male on checkout so he can work alongside her.

Other guys from school are using machetes in the produce section or driving tractors for their dads.

She is waiting for marriage, which is good for them both, she assures him.

Jim's hormones are wild, evident as much in the stubble and muscles as the pimples and moods. They steal time on weekends and sit in the bush, kissing and hugging, his fingers probing and rubbing until she sighs and shakes.

Sometimes she flinches, and he wishes she'd tell him, though he knows he doesn't want to hear it.

The night of the deb ball her father shakes Jim's hand.

I'm very proud tonight, thank you.

Jim thinks it strange, fighting between face value and scripted cynicism.

Jim receives a watch in the post from his father to celebrate the night. He realises how much the old man doesn't understand.

Jim lies on the water tank, wrapped tight against the wind that cleared his eyes. He's broken it off with the girl, after two years' torment.

He was intuitive to abuse, especially the family kind – his mum worked with enough of those kids born into hell for him to diagnose that look. The way his girlfriend's body stiffened and became taut when her older brother was present was enough to draw a conclusion. She'd told just one friend before him, a girl who a week later died in a car wreck. A tree at school grew for her. The pain. That pain Jim could understand, and for a while it was enough. But the injustice of it all made him run, as he wasn't a fighter yet.

This, his last year of high school, sees the cycling dropped, the job end, and the football peter out with his knees. School remains and Tony is there, still loyal and still economical in expectations.

On that water tank, Jim is both alone and sitting in a chamber of like minds. He hears Kurt Cobain sing and Joe read books. Even when life seemed shit the stars were limitless in the black of living by the sea, two hours drive from a city. He lay with his hands behind his head, the sound of distant surf the only stimulus but those stars. They were brilliant in every sense, wondrous and comforting for always being there.

Nigel? Only his mother calls him that, and it is thankfully less frequent.

It's Jim, Mum. J-I-M. Jim.

Okay, Jim, she says, climbing up the ladder. Thought you might want some chocolate.

Oh, yeah, Jim sits up and scoots his blanket across for his mum.

You know, I named you Nigel for a reason. She sits next to him, handing over an open block of Dairy Milk.

Yeah, I know. Jim looks out at the twinkling town, a crust along coast that stretches out below their hill.

You think of him much? His mum put a hand on his knee, lighting up a joint with one hand.

Joe? Jim was never sure if it was from the quack's direction or his parent's long-winded separation, but his mother had never broached the subject.

Yeah, Joe. Nigel Two. Jim's mum takes a drag and holds the joint out to share.

For the first time, Jim takes the offering.

Ha, well, look at you, seventeen and all grown up. I'm proud of you.

Jim draws a toke as his mum hugs him, coughing from the combination. He takes in the moonlight on the sea, the green neon cross of the town's church.

I think of him all the time, you know, Jim says. He wipes a tear to sleeve and blows a jet of smoke into the sky.

Anyway, if we hadn't of had the same names and picked new ones we would have got the shit kicked out of us – Nigel's a pretty gay name, Mum.

Yeah, sorry Jim. For everything.

His mum cries as they sit and watch the water and the stars, smoking until the cold bites.

Jim leaves home later that year and lives in the mountains. He studies and works and shares a room with a friend from his city days.

The world is different up there, the same clarity and stars, but it's the smells and the sounds that change. No she-oaks and surf, all gums and silence. It's summer again, bright but cold, movements laboured in the deserted snowfield. The couple of people in the course who own cars become friends to everyone, as once a week they pack like sardines to get off the mountain for supplies and sanity.

At a party, Jim watches a guy fall from a second-storey window, only to return to the room moments later as if he meant it. He falls two more times that night, quite the joker. Jim wonders why a guy like that is allowed to go on. Girls strive for attention and Jim finds easier, less taxing company. Beds are seldom cold but the novelty remains, and somehow he and his friend survive the frigid summer and leave the barren mountain where it is and how it should be – uninhabited but for those seeking adventure. Theirs is all full up from that place.

Back in Melbourne, Jim works in hotels to use his diploma, and searches for what's next. Before he knows it, years pass, courses and jobs blend, and he becomes a wanderer, a drifter of intellect and ambition. He tries architecture – Joe wanted to do that – but it doesn't stick: too rigid and uncompromising.

He misses the sound of the sea, forgets he likes to read.


Jim sits at the keyboard and stares at the blank screen. The cursor blinking while a Nirvana CD plays for the first time in 10 years. He needs that mood.

He is planning a speech for the next day, an anniversary for Joe. He's ready for something like that. Needs to take those final steps. Jim sits and stares, the stereo reciting words he'd never forgotten and his girlfriend's singing obliviously leaking from the other room. Grunge rock versus soprano opera. Joe would like it, a mix of air guitar and high art. Jim pictures a ten-year-old blond boy having guitar lessons from George Harrison, Maria Callas teaching him to sing in tune.

Jim knows enough prose and poetry to recite. But it is the whole of it he wants to say. The missed time as well as the memories, the loss as well as the benefit of not being there in the flesh. Jim still lives in the city, the stars all packed up, the ocean poured away. The smells and sounds industrial, the days and weeks relentless. He's gone full circle and worked a few things out, found that it all makes sense when you're having fun with someone you love. Going for a ride. Sharing some laughs. Reading a book aloud.

Jim smiles. Types.

The joy of it all, Joe. That's what you missed – that's what we had – but all that you missed … I'll tell you, Joe, I'll tell you all about it, what you had and what you left with, all that you went without: Ah, no, Joe, you never knew the whole of it …


Note – the title and final line are from a Bruce Dawe poem of the same name, from *Sometimes Gladness: Collected Poems, 1954–1987* (Longman, 1997).

This short story has previously appeared in *Griffith REVIEW Edition 13: The Next Big Thing* (2006).

# 'Soliloquy for one dead' [Criminal Featherweight Remix]
## Kirk Marshall

Jimmy Tenderfoot Butterfly's eyes – two furious oculars engineered to determine the silhouette of a gazelle secreted amongst a snarl of baobab trees whole kilometres away – were stinging from the smoke. The nicotine was obscuring his ordinarily incendiary vision as though sheets of gossamer rain, hanging heavily like the halitosis of Damocles over his monstrous forehead. He yawned, once, without much inspiration, and returned the cigarette to the crimson cushion of his mouth. Butterfly's mother had never cultivated any real appreciation for the pastime, and had failed to comprehend the value of indulging in it *especially* whilst inert and blinded by trails of silvering smoke in bed. But this was Butterfly's room – he paid her sufficient board enough, per week, to dispossess her of a chance to forget it – and if he felt the impulse to hunker against the headboard, his torso entangled in new-laundered sheets and a deck of smokes squashed into his fist like some rare blue flower, he'd occupy his morning however the fuck a sudden whim instructed. He yawned once more, and shifted his position so that one arm, his left, could extend toward last night's late-hour glass of scotch set squarely on the tallboy. His eyes caught his reflection, swimmy and prehistoric, like a bluebottle encased in amber, at the bottom of his glass. What a haggard fuck, he thought, with loathing.

There used to exist a time, during some unprecedented manifestation of my life, where I remember feeling rested. It seemed a time of populous and ungovernable good fortune, back then, when I was ten, twelve; I didn't entertain narcotic thoughts that sleep was swarming on my skin, feasting on my every reserve of energy, like a clat of leeches. I'd wrestle the bike out from beneath the neighbourly conspiracy of hedgerows with which I'd ensconced it, glowing mint like the gold in a huckster's dentures, and burst astride it down the footpath, my feet pounding squeakily at the pedals, reverberant with squash-court sounds. The entire phalanx of weatherboard terrace-houses would wheel past me. Their shapes, taut and white, like bed-linen hung on the line fanned flat by a serendipitous wind. Tony Moretti would already be folded at the threshold to the local convenience store, anticipating Butterfly's scandalous entrance, the tread of his ten-gear's tyres igniting industrial sparks as he slammed the breaks and whirligigged through the shop-front gravel. Moretti, hands furled into fists and abandoned to their own devices within the pockets of his grey denim jacket, would merely nod, offer a paltry acknowledgement of Butterfly's extravagant risk, and would transfer the Lucky Strike behind his ear to his lower lip.

Sordid twelve-year-old badasses, us, they were swift to self-promote. Theirs was no counterfeit gamble, no spurious bravura: they were unopposed gallants and braver than a lame dog in rattlesnake country, south-city grommets of a twin design, tiny men with cowboy hearts capable of catastrophe. It wasn't an especially remarkable circumstance to observe Butterfly and Moretti loitering with their fable-and-motorcycle haircuts, Lost Boys as channelled by River Phoenix, on the adobe-and-concrete stoop of the local corner store. 'You *motherfucker*,' Moretti would crow, matter-of-factly, as though taxonomising an altogether new species. 'I mean it. Did she ask you to romance her away from her kitchen chores? Or is there some alternate reason why I've been waiting *half-an-hour* to see your fucking thumb-face emerge 'round that street corner?'

Butterfly, even then a measured and generous man, would have to later concede, in retrospect, that his own face did share a certain verisimilitude to a knuckle, his head's architecture as devoid of a contour as a rooftop radiator. He had the implacable countenance of a varlet, taciturn and ridiculous – a head like a hearse, really, with just as much character and colour. Moretti, in contrast, maundered about Melbourne with features of a continental construction, a Ferrari in dishwater denim, with a laugh like the scream of axles on sidewalk, brazen and accelerative. But he would not admit as much to his friend in person. That would only result in putting an end to the game, invite a stranglehold on their precocious teenage need to best one another. No moment shared between them would ever constitute a morally appropriate exchange whereby Butterfly came clean, and admitted that Moretti was on the money: his really was a chimerical exterior; he *was* an ugly Frankensteinian fuck. So he contained the dark truth of that knowledge, bottled it up and buried it in the soil beneath the violet tangle of his voice. Said: 'In point of fact, yeah, Little Italy, I gots a right justification.' 'Vouch for it?' 'No sweat.' 'Go on, then, what's kept your sleepy ass?'

Even now, in his bedroom, fifteen years later and coveting his solitude, Butterfly could still see the vain star in Moretti's lapis-lazuli eye supernova into black oblivion. No twelve-year-old's *that* hard – hard enough, savage enough to endure the pageantry of hell's very own procession. Down into their fey, fallacious teenage world descended the angel of corruption, singing his madrigal for all the fallen saints and twisted darlings of that East Melbourne suburb. With rhapsody dissolving like cocaine into his bloodstream, his pulse pounding, Butterfly unsheathed his Daddy's gun from the innermost pocket of his jacket and pressed the snout to his best friend's forehead. It shone like an evil deed, right there, in his palm, it caught the light like flame behind a page, and the zebra stripes banding the barrel of the pistol were suddenly astir, a frenzy in his hand. 'This be what kept *my* sleepy ass,' Butterfly watched himself whisper down the narrow corridor of history to his horrified Italian companion. And he, now twenty-seven, could neither intervene upon nor prevent what his twelve-year-old *doppelgänger* proceeded to do: he could only watch it happen, again, filtered through decades like the nondistinct reflection in his scotch glass, as he thrust the handgun into his friend's gaping mouth, and pulled the trigger. Moretti was still crying, like a housewife in a Hitchcock film, when Butterfly straddled his BMX and made off to the committee of trees by the Yarra.

He wasn't equipped to be able to withstand passion and inner turbulence of this kind; his was a body devised for an athlete and not a thinker; his head – for five rounds, determining the most favourable side of the ring's spring-propelled floor, and a resin mouthguard. Butterfly was a professional prizefighter, had been a boxer from the get-go, and he was sharp-witted enough to understand that it was an irrevocable discipline, a sport you could not scorn or spurn, a commitment you could not turn your back on. Nonetheless, there did sporadically eventuate *dangerous days*, long ones which seemed to draw out like nails when retracted with the claw of a hammer, when he'd question his resolve – ask himself why he'd brutalised his friend in that way, renounce the light and proclaim to his coach that boxing was for jackals, for sharks, for beasts. But such a conviction wouldn't last a day – they rarely even stood up to his coach's enforced scrutiny, like a wave form which would collapse as soon as a microscope observed it – and Butterfly would be coaxed and coddled into admitting that he loved the might of the fight, Yussir, There ain't nothing more sweet than a tussle against a formidable rival, There ain't no fanny or skirt worth that calibre of motherfucking honour, *hoo*-boy, Nossuh! He had minerals, and he had pride. It was these very attributes, these indeterminable virtues, as unlearned as the nature of a prodigy, his own phylum of genius, which encouraged within all those who met Butterfly the inclination to think him a noble man. A noble man wouldn't divorce himself from his talent, in the same way that he wouldn't quit the one he loved. But undermining his every modicum of goodwill was that sour-mouthed inner voice telling him he was dispensable, disreputable, reviled and revolting. It had bloomed within him, this voice, with its singular Italian inflection, when he was just a morose teenage boy, and now it incapacitated his self-confidence at the pulse of a synapse, now its carnivorous reign meant that no happy thought could escape unmolested.

These people hate me, he'd think, pacing about the ring and hitting his skull with a glove-suited fist, as he espied the clamouring mouths and cynical gazes of the spectators from between the cage of ropes. It's just like Tony's parents, and the girls at school, and the wrath of Daddy all over again, he'd think. Sometimes he wanted to howl, and the wolf within him would break through the tree-line, so that everyone could see the rabid dance of his eyes, but most people these days associated this rage with the boxing – they didn't stop to consider with any overt sense of concern as to whether young Jimmy Tenderfoot Butterfly, up there, artfully dodging and sparring his heart out, was okay *on the inside*. And those collective coterie of watchers, week in and week out, they certainly didn't demonstrate any palpable apprehension when Butterfly ascended into the quarter-finals with electricity in his brain and confusion in his steps, confronting Joe Nigel Moretti, Tony's older brother, a man so svelte and lithe with muscle that Butterfly saw the tide wash back in. 'I'm going to fuck you,' Joe grunted with the hoarse romance of an avenging champion, 'Just like you fuck that divorcee bitch of a mother, I'm going to fuck you. Tony didn't come tonight, but he sure as shit knows I mean it.' And all the threads suddenly converged to simulate some sort of sense to Butterfly, the cinnamon smoke exhaling from Joe's bulldog mouth, the ebbtide of the Yarra river beneath the spangle of the early-nineties daylight, the inability for him to launch into the world and his prevailing sense of comfort living in his mother's sucko-stucco house, the moment he thought he glimpsed a

116

car, submerged, beneath the surface of Melbourne's living water. It had been a hearse. Yes, indeed: Butterfly could now appreciate the intricacy of the design, the web of significance with such alacrity, such newfound veracity; he'd hated Tony Moretti for being a someone with a *future*, a someone with a family and looks and indiscreetly gorgeous girlfriends and a channel out of the morass of a hard fucking childhood, he hated being the unattractive wraith at school whom everybody had to embrace as *financially disadvantaged*, he hated having a bike with a bullshit chain and the sanctuary of a slurry of brown water wending its way through the country of his lost future. If he was going to drown, a disenchanted and discontent man, he would lash himself fast to the driver's seat of that submerged fucking ghost hearse.

'What kept your sleepy ass?' Butterfly asked, with the cruel laughter of a plague of Hercules moths. 'What *kept* your sleepy ass, boy, 'coz I been waiting *fifteen* years to do what I did to your pussy brother, and put these guns to your motherfucking *head*.' The question was rhetorical; it required no enigmatic solution. Jimmy Tenderfoot Butterfly didn't anticipate an answer, not at least for another fifteen years, when the paramedic staff idled an inert and blood-spat Joe Moretti into the double-doors of the warbling ambulance outside the auditorium. Butterfly revealed the breadth of his wingspan, opened wide his aching brown arms, and retreated into the mist of a piping locker-room shower, his eyes stinging in the smoke again, a platinum belt slung over his hunched shoulder. He gazed at his reflection, swimmy and prehistoric, shimmering on the surface of the textiles. He was a winner again. Butterfly didn't look so much like a thumb, as he did the whole fist.

# The New Cage
## Stefan Laszczuk

I owned my first budgie when I lived in the first house. My bedroom was next to the family toilet. Four kids with weak, nervous bladders made for a lot of flushed awakenings during the night. I used to lie there and listen to the cistern spluttering and gurgling like a pot boiling over, as it refilled time and time again. Each time as the noise subsided, I would arch my ear, hoping for silence. Sometimes I got it, and slept. More often than not I would be kept awake by my parents' voices. Voices muffled by twelve stairs and a thirty-foot corridor of thick brown carpet, so you couldn't hear what they were saying. You could only hear they were angry. My parents' eventual and inevitable break-up was also their own painful rebirth. Embryonic friendship became foetal love became two writhing bodies forcing their way out of a cunt of a situation, to find themselves screaming and crying in a new life without each other. It was only rebirth of sorts though. My father still needs his amniotic fluid and my mother still kicks against her walls.

The worst of it was over years ago, and I can only remember the whole time as some kind of surreal road accident. A lot of speeding, swerving arguments and then suddenly, my brothers, my sister and I wandering off the side of a highway covered in blood and shock, wondering just what the hell happened and just where the hell we go from here. My father drunk and asleep at the wheel. My mother bundling him out of the car and coming back frantically to pick us up and tend to our wounds.

I used to open the cage door and let my budgie fly about the house. People said I was mad doing that in a house with four cats. I probably was a bit. Probably my extreme allergy to cats combined with the fact that I lived with four of them kept me in a sort of mad state. I didn't like those cats much. My dad hated them. His hatred for those cats must have made it slightly easier for him when he became unwelcome in our house. When the swinging lead boot of my mother the goalkeeper kicked my father straight back out of the door he rolled in. Kicked him all of three suburbs away. I bet he didn't think three suburbs seemed that far at the time, but I bet he didn't realise that it would take him longer than the rest of his life to get back. About a week after he was gone, one of the cats decided to migrate across the road. A few months ago, I bumped into the neighbour whose house it had snuck away to in those early years. She told me it had recently died in terrible pain from the cats' version of AIDS. I shrugged my shoulders at the news. My little brother had literally bawled for hours when we told him his favourite cat had left us for the Browns. I told him I would share my budgie with him. That worked out fine for about a month. Worked out fine until the budgie nosedived onto a pan of frying potatoes while we were all waiting for dinner in front of the television. Mum investigated the clatter in the kitchen to find him sizzling amongst the spuds. I waited until the ad break to identify the body. It almost seems comical now, in a charred black humour sort of way, but it wasn't particularly 'anything' to four hungry knee-highs at the time. We had already been hardened by the leaving of one cat and one father. We had pork sausages on their own for tea. And the next week I bought another budgie.

It was almost a year before I would let the second budgie out of his cage, and I only did it outside of meal times. As I was approaching my own feathery existence, my mother was beginning to let me fly about a bit too. Being a typically trustworthy teenager, I spent my weekends getting stoned with my buddies or stealing their parents' grog. I was carefree for a while. Then one night I woke up in the dark in my friend's spare bedroom. There was a man on my bed with his hands inside my underpants. When I sat up he pushed my face hard into the pillow and ran away. The whole fright lasted maybe twenty seconds, or twenty years – depending on which way you look at it. Sleeping on my own hasn't been quite the same since. Anyway, the next day I got home to find my second budgie had been attacked and killed by our crazy cat – the one that we couldn't ever get near enough to pat because we had apparently terrorised it as a kitten. The one that would eventually shit out its stomach on the kitchen floor before it died hating us.

As upset as I wanted to be about the second budgie, I was still in shock from the night before. My friend's parents hadn't believed my intruder story when I had woken them at 4:30 in the morning. They'd said it was a bad dream. Yeah, right, I thought. A bad dream that left the door open on the way out. Still, even I preferred to believe it had never really happened and told myself a dream was all it was. Two weeks later, I found out that the man came back again. This time he went next door and chloroformed the neighbours' twelve year-old boy, took him away and fucked him for three days. Then he dumped him in the park down the road. I still think about what would have happened if I hadn't have woken up that night. Anyway, I ended up telling mum what happened to me. She had too much work to do to really fix anything, but she let me sleep with the light on for a while. She didn't let me have any more budgies though. There were too many predators around, she said.

I had to wait until I moved out of home to get my third budgie. My new flatmate and her boyfriend didn't like it. The boyfriend always complained about the smell. He apparently had a very sensitive nose. As far as I was concerned the only thing he was good at sniffing out was a bargain. Within days of arriving at her tiny flat, I found that it was unofficially a home for three. I paid half the rent and the bills and he smoked a lot of dope in our lounge room. Many people wouldn't tolerate an extra person living for free in their space for seven nights a week. As it was my first share house, I did. Ironically, in the end, it was my flatmate who asked me to leave. Perhaps it was because I drank a lot. Perhaps it was because of the night I drank a lot and tried to put my hand inside her knickers. Or because of the night that I drank a lot and then interrupted their midnight sex to empty my swollen bladder on their bedroom floor. Either way, the budgie and I didn't last long in that flat. Not nearly as long, I hoped, as the lingering smell of urine on the bedroom carpet does for a sensitive nose.

The eventual death of budgie number three was nobody's fault and everybody's fault. Picture this. A family reunion of sorts. I even brought the budgie along to sit with us in the backyard at my sister's house. It was her twenty-fifth birthday. First time in nearly fifteen years we were all together in the same space, not counting hospital rooms. All four of us kids were seriously hospitalised at some stage in our lives. Mum and Dad would tolerate each other's presence for our sake then, but it wasn't exactly a cheery atmosphere. This day, however, everybody put their personal grievances aside for a couple of hours and seemed determined to sit it out peacefully. It was all very dormant, even slightly enjoyable, until my brother noticed my budgie sitting out in the open air on the side of a cracked pot. My sister's desperate lunge was only enough to serve as a sort of push. The budgie exploded up into the air and disappeared over the neighbour's fence. Our far-knit little community formed a search party.

We searched fervently for two things. One: the budgie. Two: someone to blame. Eventually we gave up on the futile birdcalls. Instead, futile blame-laying became the order of the day. As for the budgie, he probably became lunch of the day for some hungry moggie. Or perhaps he managed to avoid the cats and starve to death instead. I never knew what happened to him when he disappeared over that fence. I just knew he wasn't coming back. Unable to find someone to blame, the members of the search party settled for telling each other to get lost. Then we each disappeared back over our own fences.

Quite a few years passed before I bought my fourth budgie. I bought him when I moved into a flat of my own. He's still alive and seems happy enough. A little nutty, I suppose, from staring at himself in a swinging mirror for the last six years. But then, I guess we all get like that. He's a feisty little bugger and he knows how to work his beak. Changing his food and water trays means getting near him, means pain. In a couple of years there won't be much of the hand that feeds him left to bite. It hurts, but I like his style, admire it even. I always open the cage for him to fly around, but it's a privilege that, unlike my previous birds, he seems indifferent to. He barely leaves his perch. Now and then he'll unleash a flurried blizzard of tiny feathers as he makes a quick bolt around the main room, but he never stays out long. The budgie and flying is like a fat guy and jogging. He's what you might call a perch potato. He seems fairly content, but I've always felt guilty about the size of his cage. So two weeks ago on my birthday, I bought him a new one.

The new cage was black. It was easily three times as tall and twice as wide as his old one. The bars ran horizontally around it, instead of vertically. To a human, this gave it less of a sense of being jail-like. To a budgie, I don't think it made a difference. The new cage had three perches, unlike the old cage with its well-worn lone roost. Also, you could open it right up. Even the roof folded outwards in two halves so that the budgie could take straight off into the air and fly if it wanted to. The front panel of the cage could be unlatched so that it swung completely open, removing all visual barriers in front of the perch. The food and water trays were big enough for a family of small pigs, let alone a single bird. There were mirrors and bells everywhere. In the corner, a huge branch of gum leaves hung down, alongside a massive slab of compressed seed and honey. The perch potato would be in heaven.

At least he would be eventually. To get to a heaven, I guess the budgie first had to believe in a god. And that god was me. A god that had just been to a birthday dinner with his father and his father's verging-on-illegally-young girlfriend. A god that had got drunk to the point of telling his father to stick his life-after-thirty advice up his cancer-ridden colon, and her to stick her life-in-general advice wherever she stuck old men's cocks. A god that had broken two bottles as he struggled to grab the rest of the beer from their fridge. That had held his bleeding finger hard against his earlobe so he could hear the cab phone operator over the wailing and the shouting. That had given up trying to hear anything and just walked home.

I suppose it didn't help that I tripped over with the cage in the dark when I got back to my room. The noise of me sprawling across the floor and my bottle smashing in the corner was more than enough to put the budgie on the alert. After that, it took me about two hours of slurred coaxing to realise that the six years of trust I thought I had built up with the budgie amounted to squat. Apparently I wasn't even his friend, let alone his master, let alone his god. I was bloodshot eyes and dried-blood ear stuck to a sweaty pale face swaying on a chair. I was endless cigarettes and coughing up of lungs.

The budgie sat cautiously, a little defiantly, at the opposite end of his tiny white cage, while I leered through tobacco smoke like a cat at a mouse hole. My initial tender attitude soon gave way to drunken apathy. I decided to simply reach in and pull the little bugger out. It's the best thing for him, I told myself. I had never tried it before, though I suspected, and I believe the budgie did too, that it would be a simple enough task to grab him. I deliberately tried not to use too much force. I didn't want to scare him shitless. I had grown quite close to the ball of feathers over the years and I didn't want him dying of a panic-related heart attack.

I should have been more firm. Each half-hearted grab only resulted in a panicked flurry of feathers and a shrill scared click of the throat. The only things I managed to hold on to were his beautiful tail feathers. The sight of them caught in my own bloody fingers made me stop. After all, the whole idea was to *not* freak the budgie out. I wrapped a strip of my shirt around the bleeding and sat down to think of another less tail-feathers-caught-in-bloody-fingers way. Then it struck me like a dull, throbbing pulse.

I placed the budgie's old cage on top of the new one, both with doors open. Then I gradually began removing all of his landmarks. First, the food and water trays which I put on the floor of the new cage. Then I cut the wires that held his little loft bed of three sticks which I then individually dragged out of the cage or snapped as required. Next went his red mirror with its tiny bell. Last of all, I gently reached in and removed the perch he was sitting on. He hopped away as I dragged it slowly through the door, until he got to the end and simply dropped down to the cage floor. I backed off and let him stand there in the empty cage, among the sand and his own shit. Perhaps out of resignation, or simply out of curiosity, he almost immediately poked his little head out of the front door and started climbing to the top of his cage. As soon as he was out, I shut the door and held the cage with him perched on top, in front of his new home. Quick as a flash he jumped inside. I shut his door, locked my door and stumbled to bed.

After much tossing and turning it was the next day. My drawn curtains would have rendered the room dark, except that I had fallen asleep with the TV on again. I still couldn't get used to sleeping alone in total darkness. Through a flickering haze I awoke to see the budgie sitting quietly on the perch. Usually by this time he would be singing me awake, or at least fluttering around a bit. There was nothing. He just perched there and stared at me like I'd stolen his home.

Over the last two weeks he has made feeble, pathetic attempts to access his new food bin. He used to be able to slide down his vertical bars to the food below. It isn't possible with the horizontal ones. He has to step cautiously, weighing up every move for a few seconds before he continues his descent. Now and then he slips and plunges to the cage floor where he chirps in dismay and rights himself with all the fumbling grace of a three-day old chick. I don't know if it's deliberate or not. All I know is that it makes me feel very guilty. He's completely ruined my present, the selfish bastard. He has a bigger cage. More room. More playthings. More doors to get in and out. He's supposed to love it. Instead, he's thrown himself into defiant depression. And so here I am, dancing like a naked muppet to the sounds of the new Tom Waits album, hoping to cheer my fourth budgie up. And I'm wondering if a budgie could actually die of depression, and I'm really hoping not. And I'm wondering what people would make of this if they saw me springing around my room naked. I'm wondering whether they would still say I was mad. But I know they won't see me or say anything. Because you can't see through locked doors and drawn curtains.

# Again, the Healing Tickle (the Way Black Glitters): A mash-up

## Angela Meyer

The man has Don Henley hair, reflected in the tram window. A skinny bit-piece, a diet mainly composed of fragments, the way you blink and miss things. Meals get around him this way. He gets off and leaves his stench. I'm left wondering whether to eye the hot piece or not. She seems to be avoiding my eye. Heaven's below.

It's my last lecture. Ever. By choice. My ambitions have fluttered to the ground, like scratched-off dandruff flakes. I can no longer believe in Heathcliff as avenging entrepreneur in shiny boots. My boots are cracked like polar caps. They will always shun the shine. It isn't their style.

I decide not to daydream past my stop like I have three times before, because I'm old. But every time I lock on a building, another face murmurs, in memory or shaped by fingertips and tongues. Another woman in front of me. And between all the people, the absences, and sharks at their backs, making them hunch or dive into their fantasy novel.

I stand up in time with ghosts and step out. The tram's electric crackle lights up the cloudy sky. It's the dead bus, which glides on black tracks, and sucks vehemently at contentedness.

The headache of time for reflection.

The last lecture, and I'll see her – rainbow assortment of animal bones. Wish again to take her to a shanty far from shanty town, scrape an orange plastic chair along the sand and sit her on it, no need to kick against those breezy walls. Nature would be wild and alien, and our feathery existence would be among the noblest.

I notice, as she pulls out her folder, the misshapen arms. They aren't of the anxiety of influence. *Oh Virginia*, she says to her friend in the way Leonard does. She says that metafiction is a well worn path, but it is still magic. The lumpen silhouette of an author narrates us. I hear the construction behind me – a whirr and click of clockwork. Her pinkness is ghosting before my eyelids. Shit the dream.

If only she could see the swinging mirror before her. But my teeth are black around the edges from cigarettes, and she is distracted by the pretty bells everywhere. It is my last chance. Her orgasm would be compressed honey. Mine would be the cock of an old man. Bloodshot eyes and dried-blood ear. Never knew what I was doing here in the first place. They ignore me, look away at my click of the throat.

But the ache for her ornate cornices, the ability of tongue-and-groove that comes with time. Dovetailing to her secrets, the way she wants the boys to. They are merely an assemblage of confused rods and pistons.

Big explosion. Lost bits. Stroll around the garden and the wind gusting across the roof. The adrenalin wasn't useful. Perhaps I was too forceful. Another broad on the tram back has *her* hair without her peachiness, she'd leave a coppery aftertaste. The moon suddenly weighs nothing. Black tracks. I escape into the night, deserted and glittering. At least I tried, said a small knowing smile. Desire drips like liquid from my face. There is a bar around the corner, with no one I know. *Midnight Cowboy* on the TV in the corner, a bull's head hung, contrasted by mirror ball.

Feeling guilty. Love? No. A bombsite of the sky. Bisexual people stacked and upended inside. My own sensibilities rotten. The music percussive but my limbs sagging. The TV stand with a web of wires perched upon it like a crown. Cataloguing the sip that keeps me going, on a bar stool, a pedestal. Countless assorted seconds I have left. Not bereft of essence but needing to pour liquid into gaps. The puncture would only last a day or two, then scab over like the others, the process tickling. A new supple will come along, maybe not so young this time, perhaps made of bronze.

Looking around the room – simulacrum. Fat old men in untucked shirts. Many would laugh at my going back to uni. They'd be renovating houses, fishing for trout, watching pert bicycle buttocks but not trying. Many would have wives, once white slenderbeams, now wrinkled but accepting. Old mate raises his schooner to me when he catches my daydream. I raise one back.

# Biographical Information

**Michelle Almirón** is a Melbourne writer stranded in Oxford with her husband for the next two years. She is an emerging novelist who was awarded a mentorship with Christos Tsiolkas through the Arts Council, a Varuna Manuscript Development Masterclass with Creative Director, Peter Bishop, as well as being long-listed for the Vogel Award. She has published short stories, articles and scholarly pieces in print and on the internet. Courageously, she is now working on two novels: *Disappearing*, the story of Erica who discovers her true identity suppressed by the clandestine activities of her parents, and *Flesh*, the story of a debauched addiction.

**Amy Barker** (Ed.) was winner of the 2008 Queensland Premier's Literary Award for Best Emerging Author. Her first novel, *Omega Park*, will be published by University of Queensland Press (UQP) in 2009. Amy is Project leader of *Remix My Lit* (www.remixmylit.com). She is based in Brisbane. Visit amybarkeronline.com

**Lee Battersby** is the multi-award winning author of over seventy stories in Australia, the US and Europe, including appearances in such markets as 'Year's Best Fantasy & Horror', 'Year's Best Australian SF & Fantasy' and 'Writers of the Future'. His collection *Through Soft Air* is available via Prime Books. He lives in Perth, Western Australia, with his wife, writer Lyn Battersby, and three children. He blogs at battersblog.blogspot.com

**Phillip A. Ellis** is an external student studying English Honours at the University of New England. His poetry collection, *The Flayed Man*, has been published by Gothic Press (www.gothicpress.com). Another will be published by Hippocampus Press, who published his concordance to the poetry of Donald Wandrei (www.hippocampuspress.com/other/collected-poetry-and-prose-poems-of-donald-wandrei.html). He is the editor of AustralianReader.com (australianreader.com/index.php), Similax (similax-poetry.blogspot.com), and Melaleuca. His webpage is at www.geocities.com/phillipellis01/

**Ashley Hauenschild** is embroiled in the final year of a Bachelor of Arts (Creative Writing, Philosophy) at the University of Queensland, and shall feel jolly pleased when he graduates. *Remix My Lit* is the first published work he has contributed to. When not involved in remixing literature, he revolves elliptically around Brisbane's improvised – and premeditated – comedy cliques.

**Cate Kennedy** lives in Victoria's north east. She is the author of a travel memoir (*Sing and Don't Cry: A Mexican Journal*; Transit Lounge), two collections of poetry (*Signs of Other Fires*, 2001, and *Joyflight*, 2004) and a collection of short stories, *Dark Roots*, (Scribe Publications). Her work has appeared widely in Australia, in the US and the UK. She is currently at work on her first novel, *The World Beneath*, scheduled for publication in September 2009. She's also working on a stage play based on the Queen's Royal Tour of Australia in 1954, hopefully to be performed in a CWA hall near you in early 2010.

**Stefan Laszczuk** is currently undertaking a PhD in Creative Writing from the University of Adelaide. He recently won the 2007 Vogel Award for his second novel, *I Dream of Magda*. His first novel, *The Goddamn Bus of Happiness*, was the winner of the South Australia Festival of Literature Award for an unpublished manuscript. He also won the SA Writers' Centre short story competition in 2002, which resulted in the publication of a book of short stories entitled *The New Cage*. Stefan currently lives in Melbourne, and is working on another novel.

**Mark Lawrence** is a writer, editor and blogger who writes mainly non-fiction and essays and dabbles in taking photographs. Mark lives in Melbourne's northern suburbs with his partner and two young sons. He has published his blog (marklawrence.blogspot.com) on a Creative Commons license since 2004. His 'Live Fed Square Remix' is his first published work of fiction.

**Matthew Lowe** is a Brisbane writer. A recipient of the 2005 Express Media Mentorship Award, his work has appeared in *Griffith REVIEW*, *Idiom 23* and in titles by Cleis Press. In 2007 his short story 'Endless Against Amber' was runner-up in the Josephine Ulrick Literature Prize.

**Emily Maguire** is the author of three novels – *Smoke in the Room*, *The Gospel According to Luke* and *Taming the Beast* – and *Princesses and Pornstars*, a work of non-fiction. Her articles and essays on sex, religion, culture and literature have been published widely including in *The Sydney Morning Herald*, *The Age* and *The Observer*.

**Kirk Marshall** is the Brisbane-born(e), Melbourne-based author of *A Solution to Economic Depression in Little Tokyo, 1953*, a 2007 Aurealis Award-nominated full-colour illustrated graphic novelette. He holds a Bachelor of Creative Industries (Creative Writing), with Distinction from the

Queensland University of Technology, and a first-class Honours degree in Professional Writing from Deakin University. In 2009, he is a non-fiction columnist for ISM: online, an international think-tank for creative youth, a panellist for the Emerging Writers' Festival, and editor of Red Leaves, Australia's only English-language/Japanese bi-lingual literary journal www.myspace.com/redleaveskoyo

**Damian McDonald** was born in Canberra, in 1969. He grew up in domestic disharmony and poverty, but found inspiration in rock music. He moved to Sydney at age sixteen in the hope of beginning a career as a rock musician, but after ten years of loud, hard living, decided it was time to think about another career – one with a regular salary attached. He returned to the ACT to begin studying a BA in Communication at the University of Canberra – where he won the William Heinemann Australia Prize for the most promising first-year student in Professional Writing – but found that Sydney suited him far better, and so completed a BA in English Literature at the University of Western Sydney, and then an MA in Creative Writing at the same institution. He has been unable to give up playing guitar and writing songs though, and still performs with his band The MakeUp. Damian's manuscript *Luck in the Greater West* won the 2007 ABC Fiction Award and the novel was published in October 2007 by ABC Books. He has also had poems and short stories published in university journals. Damian currently works at the Powerhouse Museum in Sydney as a curator, but has held positions, unfortunately, in retail and wholesale.

**Angela Meyer** has had fiction, reviews and interviews published in *Lip, Hecate, Cordite, The Sex Mook, Southerly, Sketch, The Death Mook, Wet Ink* and others. She blogs about all things bookish for Crikey (blogs.crikey.com.au/literaryminded), and is the editorial assistant at *Bookseller+Publisher* magazine in Melbourne.

**Scott-Patrick Mitchell** is a poet and writer living in Perth, Western Australia. He edits the thoroughly modern *MoTHER [has words ...]* zine (myspace.com/motherhaswords), a national publication which show-cases the emerging talent bristling and bubbling away in WA. He also writes music, fashion and arts articles for local community newspaper *OUTinPerth*. Scott-Patrick loves remixing, and touts Jeff Noon's *Cobralingus* as one of his all time favourite reference books.

**Philip Neilsen** is a Brisbane poet and fiction writer and a professor of creative writing at QUT. His short stories have appeared in a wide number of anthologies and journals. He has also written five fiction books for young adults and children and five books of poetry. His most recent book is *Without an Alibi* (Cambridge: Salt Publishing, 2008). He has received a CBC Notable Australian Book award, an Australia Council Writer's Fellowship and been shortlisted for an Aurealis award, among others.

**Amra Pajalic** was born in 1977. Her first novel *The Good Daughter* will be published in May 2009 by Text Publishing. Her short stories 'Siege' and 'F**k Me Eyes' have appeared in the 2004 and 2005 *Best Australian Short Stories*. *The Good Daughter* was shortlisted in the 2007 Victorian Premier's Award for an Unpublished Manuscript by an Emerging Writer. She lives in St Albans, Melbourne, with her husband, daughter and three cats. Visit amrapajalic.com

**James Phelan** is a twenty-nine-year-old Melbourne-based novelist. He holds a MA in Writing and is a PhD candidate at Swinburne University of Technology, where he has tutored. His first book was *Literati: Australian Contemporary Literary Figures Discuss Fear, Frustrations and Fame* (John Wiley & Sons 2005). His thriller novels follow NY based investigative journalist Lachlan Fox into different global hot spots and depict current affairs and geo-political themes. Fox novels include *Fox Hunt* (Hachette 2006), *Patriot Act* (2007), *Blood Oil* (2008), *Liquid Gold* (2009). James has written for a variety of newspapers and magazines and has contributed to short story anthologies and serialised novels. He is currently working on two more Lachlan Fox novels, a young-adult fiction series, and a follow up to *Literati*.

**Amelia Schmidt** has recently completed her Bachelor's degree in English, Art History and Film Studies. She is currently working on ABC's website *Pool*, running a music and arts blog, teaching music and English, freelancing as a journalist and photographer and reading lots of books. She hopes to put on a photography exhibition this year and write as many short stories as she can. She plays in a band sometimes, and in her spare time fights crime in disguise.

**Tess Toumbourou** recently returned from a year living in Indonesia to begin her Honours thesis, making sense of the chaos of the social world. She is a fiction, non-fiction and poetry writer, has written on issues such as skin whitening, as well as art reviews and prose poetry. She is working up the courage to release her drawer full of short stories into the world.

**Kim Wilkins** is a Brisbane writer of twenty novels, across numerous genres, for adults, young adults, and children. She lectures in writing at the University of Queensland, and in the community. Her novel *The Veil of Gold* was recently named best fantasy novel in the American Library Association's reading list awards.

**Sean Williams** is the author of over thirty books and seventy short stories, the latter most recently collected in *Magic Dirt: The Best of Sean Williams*. He writes for young readers as well as adults across several genres, and has been known to pen the odd dodgy haiku. His novelisation of *Star Wars: The Force Unleashed* was the first game-related tie-in to debut at #1 on the New York Times hardback bestseller list. He lives in Adelaide with his family, and DJs in his spare time.

**Danielle Wood** is the author of the Vogel Award-winning *The Alphabet of Light and Dark* and *Rosie Little's Cautionary Tales for Girls*. She lectures in English and creative writing at the University of Tasmania.

**Sarah Xu** is an artist, writer, director, full-time parent and student. Her main distraction at present is the completion of her practice-based PhD looking at gender, art and web 2.0, to which her remix of 'Alchymical Romance' contributed. Sarah's cyberfeminist artwork can be viewed on her PhD project blog fiftytwoacts.wordpress.com. Most of her cyberfeminist work, published under the pseudonym Sajbrfem, is available for use and remix under Creative Commons licenses.